The Urbana Free Library

To renew: call **217-367-4057**
or go to **urbanafreelibrary.org**
and select **My Account**

SNAKES & STONES

LISA FOWLER

Sky Pony Press
New York

Sky Pony Press books may be purchased in bulk at special discounts for sales promotion, corporate gifts, fund-raising, or educational purposes. Special editions can also be created to specifications. For details, contact the Special Sales Department, Sky Pony Press, 307 West 36th Street, 11th Floor, New York, NY 10018 or info@skyhorsepublishing.com.

Sky Pony® is a registered trademark of Skyhorse Publishing, Inc.®, a Delaware corporation.

Visit our website at www.skyponypress.com.

Books, authors, and more at www.skyponypressblog.com.

10 9 8 7 6 5 4 3 2 1

Library of Congress Cataloging-in-Publication Data is available on file.

Cover design by Georgia Morrissey
Cover illustration credit Chris Piascik

Print ISBN: 978-1-5107-1031-3
Ebook ISBN: 978-1-5107-1032-0

Printed in the United States of America

For Sarah

CONTENTS

1

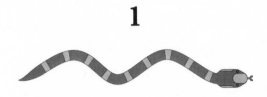

Stealing Money and Telling Lies

There hasn't been a traveling salesman in this neck of the woods in more than two years; that's what some in the crowd are saying. You'd think the folks in this Podunk town would be happy we've come, but they're not. Matter of fact, by the sound of the ruckus, they're fixing to run us out of the county. Maybe even clean off the map.

"Charlatans! Snake oil peddlers! Hoodlums! Swindlers!"

They're mad, I tell you, and getting madder by the minute.

They're brash and loud with their shouts, thrashing our wagon with sticks and branches, slinging stones that thump and thud and make hollow sounds against the old wooden red and white circus wagon.

"Chestnut Hill, keep them babies inside!" Daddy hollers. Around us, we hear crashing as the elixir bottles stacked on the side of the wagon shatter.

1

I'm crouched in the corner of the wagon, huddled on top of the triplets the same way a mother hen would gather her brood up and under her wings for protection—way too much responsibility for an ordinary twelve-year-old in a dirty, torn dress, frumpled hair, and shoes with holes in them the size of Missouri. Especially a girl that's been snatched from her mama against her will.

The wagon shimmies like warm jelly when Daddy slams the wooden flap down on the side, and it makes me feared that the wooden pegs holding it together will pop clean out of their grooves at any second. With one swift thud, he shoves the bolt across the flap, and takes off running, his black patent leather shoes making a slapping sound against the weathered brick pavers of the street. If there ever was a doubt, it's gone now. We're up to our earlobes in trouble.

My leg muscles ache from wanting to run. With every stone and bottle and stick that's hurled and bounced off the side of the wagon, I jump and dodge worse than a late-evening gnat being chased by an angry hand, same as I would if I was on the outside and every last one of them was hurled straight toward me.

I hear those familiar shoe slaps again and know Daddy's close, and as much as it pains me to admit it, just the thought brings me comfort.

Breathing deep comes easier too as I hear Daddy's voice offering up some soothing words to our horse, Old Stump. I reckon surely the wagon will rock from side to side as he climbs aboard and plops down on the wooden seat behind her, but it don't. Daddy is still on the ground with the mob, and that shoves fear even deeper into my belly.

Fuzzy-headed Hazel—stubborn as a donkey knee-deep in a manure patch and still way too much a baby at seven—is sobbing again, only this time them sobs aren't silent. This time they're weeping and wailing sobs. Sobs to wake up all the corpses in the graveyard sobs. Moaning, howling, blubbering bawls of sobs.

Makes me want to slap the sob right out of her.

But I don't.

I can't.

I'm not a slapper.

"Chestnut, you're smothering me!" Mac says with a lisp that I reckon he'll never outgrow.

"Hush up, you. You'll think smothering if that angry mob turns us over and spills us out," I say, trying as best I can to hold to the wooden walls and protect the triplets. "They'll beat the living tarnation out of the lot of us if they get their hands on us."

"I don't care. I can't breathe!"

I pull back just enough to let in a bit of air but still hold them close.

"We didn't do nothing wrong!" Hazel throws her head back and wails.

"Humph! We did too," I say, soft enough so's only a bedbug could hear. "We stole their money and told them lies."

Without some sort of help, Daddy alone with that mob don't stand a chance. Filbert must have thought it too because just at that second he breaks my grip, jumps to his feet, and eyes the door.

"Where are you going?" I holler.

Filbert, with his autumn leaf–brown hair and eyes the color of a stormy sky, moves closer to the door. Tears as big as baseballs roll the length of his dimpled cheeks.

"Daddy needs help. Can't you hear them people? They'll kill him!"

"Get back here!" I snatch for him even though he's well beyond my grasp. "I said get back here now! Filbert!"

"Let me be, Chestnut," he yells, his eyes wide and darting back and forth.

With arms flailing and teeth clenched, he's more a caged animal than a worried boy in back of a wagon. Mama always said he was blessed with more guts than brains, and I reckon he's proving that more with each passing day.

"You didn't see their faces like I did," he says. "If we don't help, Daddy's sure to take a walloping from that mob."

He swipes at a cheek with his sleeve but does nothing about the leaking from his nose threatening to sneak past his lips and into his mouth. Slinging wide the double doors, he bolts like lightning down the steps, his mission-bag shirt untucked and wrinkled like he's slept in it a month, and his pants practically threadbare at the knees.

Instantly I know my hide's going to catch the devil from Daddy, but there's nothing I can do now 'cept stand here crouching, trying to protect the other two.

Straining to hear, I can pick out Filbert's war whoops from among the crowd. If I'd ever wished to be in two places at once it's now, but wishing never did make things so. I'll just have to hope and pray that Filbert has the good sense to take care of himself out there.

And as for Daddy, I say let him take a walloping. It might just do him good. Anyway, it serves him right for forcing us to help with his lying, cheating schemes.

But just as quick as those thoughts come to sloshing around in my head, even more thoughts come beating down the door to my heart.

Chestnut Hill, that's your daddy out there. That crowd'll kill him if they get the chance, and now's their chance. What in the world are you thinking? Get up off this floor and help your poor old daddy right now!

Mama says the worst thing a body can be is conflicted, and with both the good and the bad thoughts sloshing together in my brain, I reckon you could say that conflicted is exactly what I am. Reckon all that's left is to figure out which of them conflicting thoughts to listen to—the head thoughts, or the heart's.

"Stay here!" I shout, jumping up and flinging an out-stretched finger toward trembling Mac and blubbering Hazel.

Stopping just inside the doors of the wagon, I hesitate, studying the lay of the land. To the left, under the wide open arms of a stubby young sycamore, a crowd is gathered like angry bees around a hive. There are even children watching.

With angry fists shoved into the air, they're hollering loud and stirring up the pot. In the dusky light of early evening, even a blind groundhog could see these folks are out for blood.

The men are wadded—on the ground—flopping around on top of each other like fresh-strung fish on a creek bank, dirt flying out from among them like dust storming the prairie.

And Filbert? Well, I don't yet see my brother, but knowing him like I do, I'd say he's right down in the thick of things, in the middle of that filthy wad.

All of a sudden and just as I'm about to jump from the wagon, one of those wadded floppers comes up for a breath of fresh air. Good thing, too, otherwise I might never have laid eyes on my brother—hanging on for dear life with one hand gripped to the back of that man's shirt, clobbering him in the head and hollering, "You get off my daddy right now!"

Clearly the man's a discombobulated mess, but Filbert's hanging on, the same as he would if he was being bucked by a wild horse.

Jumping off the back of the wagon, I scoop up the first stick with a promise.

Whack!
Whack!
Whack! Whack!

I'm taking out wadded floppers faster than a bullfrog sucking up skeeters, and every single one I swat stands up, grabs his head, and staggers around like he's not got a clue of what's hit him.

Just as I pull way back on my stick, searching for my next flopper, something grabs hold to my arm.

"I don't mean tomorrow or the next day either. Tonight, you hear?"

"I hear," Daddy mumbles.

The lawman props one hand on his pistol and wiggles his fingers over top, like he's just itching to pull that gun from his holster and give it a fire. Mama says the only thing worse than a lawman with an itchy finger is a cantankerous newborn with the colic. Both get your nerves in a wad.

Filbert stares at Daddy, shifting his weight to one leg—just like Daddy. He squints, makes his lips form a straight line, and gives the lawman the evil eye.

"I mean it now," the lawman says, ignoring Filbert's glares. "Get on up and out of here. If I come by this way again and see your wagon or that snake oil nonsense you're shoving at innocent folks, I'll haul you in and book you. You'll be looking at no less than a week from the inside of a jail cell, understand?"

He sets his eyes to the top of Daddy's head.

Daddy scoops his hat from under the wagon, slaps it against his leg a time or two, and motions Filbert and me back up this stairs. His shoulders are slumped and saggy and he's shuffling from one foot to the other faster than a monkey standing in the middle of a bonfire. Even a half-blind squirrel at the top of a tree could see that this lawman's got Daddy agitated.

With his fingers wrapped around his hat so tight his knuckles are the color of lamb's wool and him so twitchy and jumpy, I've got a feeling my daddy would give up everything he owns right at this minute in order to be able to just take off and go to running.

I don't hesitate. I've seen that look from Daddy before, and he's not playing, so, for the second time tonight, I give Filbert a shove and follow him into the wagon, bolting the door behind us.

"Is Daddy all right?" Mac asks, his lisp ringing out like church chimes with that first "s" he utters. His face is twisted in a worried-son sort of way, and I realize that for all his fun and games, Mac was born to be the worrier for the lot of us.

I nod.

Hazel, curled in a ball on her cot, is trembling so I think she'll roll off and flop on the floor any minute. There's nothing to do but reach down and pull her close.

Instantly she uncurls, crawls into my lap, and grips me around the neck as tight as a boa constrictor. Thank goodness she's stopped her weeping and wailing—for now at least.

"What are we going to do, Chestnut?" she asks, snubbing and sniffing, making more sounds than a one-man band.

I shrug. "Reckon we'll be for getting out of town like the lawman said. Otherwise, Daddy will end up in jail."

"I don't want our daddy to go to jail." Hazel's chin and bottom lip quiver with every word. "Do you?" She cradles my face in her hands, lifting my chin to look into my eyes. "Do you, Chestnut?" she repeats. "Do you want Daddy to go to jail?"

I stare at her for the longest time without responding, happy when Mac finally speaks up and shatters the silence.

"For two years now folks have been letting their lawmen run us out of town. Why do people hate us anyway?" With a quick whipping motion, he tosses the muddy water–colored hair from his brown eyes.

Trying to be as careful as I can of my words, I hesitate. Mac's asking an awfully grown-up question for a seven-year-old.

"Humph. Well," I say, as cautious as a one-legged lady on an icy pond, "I don't think they hate us as much as they hate what we do."

The wagon jerks backwards, and by that I know we're on our way out of town. Old Stump's clipping along in a run, so I reckoned Daddy must be fierce afraid of that lawman.

"But all we're doing is entertaining them," Hazel says, pitiful-like and whiny. And all the while she's curling my raven-wing hair loosely around her finger. "You know, just like Daddy says, giving them a good show for their money. Along with, well . . . you know . . ."

She shrugs, her words trailing into nothingness, then cups her free hand around her mouth and leans in close. "You know," she whispers into my ear, "the stuff."

"The elixir," I say, pulling away. "It's elixir, Hazel. It's all right to call it what it is, you know." I shake my head until her finger lets loose of my hair. "But folks don't like to be lied to, and that's what we're doing. At least, that's what Daddy's making us do. Lie."

"Chestnut Eleanora Hill?" Daddy hollers. "Get up here. Now."

Mama says penning a middle name to a young'un is solely for the purpose of giving them fair warning as to how much trouble they're in. Reckon you might say I'm in a heap of trouble, and it just ain't right, I tell you. A girl ought to set a good example for her kin.

I stand, gently pushing Hazel back onto her cot, and smooth down the front of my dress. I don't look any of the three of them in the eyes, but reckon I don't need to. They know what's coming, same as me.

"Yes, sir?"

I lean forward and peek through the door.

"Sit."

He bobs his head toward the seat, and I notice right off that his face is as red as a rooster's comb. His hair, the color of rotting teeth, is unusually mussed and unkempt.

"Yes, sir."

I crawl out and plop down on the seat beside Daddy, but I don't look his way. There's no need. I feel his eyes, staring, looking me up and down.

Swallowing the hot liquid that's rising over and over again in my throat, I grip the wooden seat so tight my fingertips go numb.

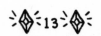

Silence rolls over the front of that wagon so thick that if I could put pencil to paper, I would draw it like the jagged side of a steep rocky canyon on a frosty January morning. And it's not a silence I've felt before in my twelve years of living. It's a separating, dividing sort of quiet, cold and harsh and unfeeling.

Daddy don't like the silence—seeing as how he's an orphan and all. From the way he tells it, there wasn't a second of silence in that orphanage he grew up in. Mama said the only reason he wanted to have so many babies in the first place is because he wanted the house to always be full of racket and noise.

After what seems like hours, I'm reckoning he's so caught up in the road and the stillness of it all, he's forgot I'm here, so I swallow down to my toes and muster up the courage to speak.

"Daddy, I—"

"Hush."

I shudder, look away fast, and clamp down on my tongue, making it impossible for words to leak out without me knowing.

Old Stump clomps along the dirt-packed road in the darkness at a slower pace than before, with nothing but the shining of the round full moon with its smeared colors of cabbage moths and snowy-white Easter lilies to light the way.

The air is strangely cool for mid-July, and my stomach's rumbling louder than a pack of wild cats trying to claw their way out of a well. But it's not from the lack of food. It's from the fear of my daddy's rebuke.

Daddy don't say a word, and for the longest time we ride in a cumbersome, clumsy sort of silence. With nothing to do but count the bushes and trees along the road, my mind starts painting, mixing in the navies and sapphires and midnight blues that all slosh together in one bucket to make up the purply black of the night sky. Cobwebby trees stretch across the dirt road like the gnarly hands of an old man reaching up, praying to be snatched into another world by his maker. What I wouldn't give for just one set of fancy paints and brushes and a scratchy ivory canvas so that I could paint the colors of the night.

The bumping up and down of the wagon jolts me back to the problem at hand. Snatching a look at Daddy, I feel a hot anger billowing from his nostrils, like a bull, warming up for a fight. He's mad all right, but what he's not got a clue of is that I'm fuming too, and keeping my anger shoved down inside is causing me a fierce displeasure. I don't like the lying Daddy wants me to do, but what's worse is that he's making me lie in front of the triplets. And it don't take more than just thinking about it to set my rage to boiling, ready to splatter out all over top of him.

Old Stump clomps along in a steady rhythm until there's not hide nor hair of a store or a barn or even a house with a tiny light flickering somewhere off in the distance, and I know by the looks of things we've crossed over the county line

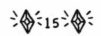

from Chattanooga. Only Daddy knows where we're headed from here, and he's not telling.

Right about the time curiosity over what Daddy's going to do to me for stirring up strife among the family takes over my mind, the devil takes over my mouth. With too many questions to swallow down and the anger inside of me boiling up, before I realize what's happening words that I can't suck back in—even if I was a mind to—come spewing from my mouth like seeds from a round purple grape.

"This wouldn't be happening if Mama was here," I blurt out. "She'd never let the triplets stand there listening to people yelling insults at you and hurling stones and bottles. Huh! She wouldn't let me or the triplets help you tell your lies in the first place."

I fold my arms across my chest sort of proud and haughty-like.

"There now. It's out," I say. "And I'm not sorry I said it."

Expecting a bucketload of angry words, I hold my breath and wait, but Daddy don't oblige. Matter of fact he don't even so much as look in my direction.

Oh, he makes me mad!

"Filbert was out of that wagon faster than a starving fox in a hen house, and there was nothing I could say that would keep him from it," I say, feeling bolder with each word blurted out. "There ain't no way I can be in two places at once. Now maybe what I did was wrong but I made the decision to stay in the wagon with the other two, which is something you

ought to have been doing by the way. But the way I see it
you was too busy snatching up money, jumping around like a
chimpanzee in a tree, and passing out lies to—"

"Whoa."

He pulls hard on the reins and Old Stump clip-clops to a
halt.

"Get down," he whispers.

"Sir?"

"Get. Down."

He speaks through clenched teeth. With one swift move-
ment of an outstretched finger, he motions me off the wagon,
pointing to the side of the road.

I jump off, plant my feet, and lock my knees, waiting for
the rebuke to come.

Staring up into the dark Tennessee night, I glance at the
whites of his eyes—well, one eye; the other's purple. He just
sits, staring off into the distance, once in a while snatching
a look my way, but never so much as opening his mouth to
speak.

From the corner of my eye I see the wagon wobble and
there's not a doubt in my mind what's making it happen.
Filbert, Macadamia, and Hazelnut are stirring, moving close
as they can get to the front, so they can hear what's about to
take place.

Daddy clears his throat and opens his mouth like he's fixing to speak, but then shuts it back before any words can leak
out.

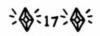

He leans over and spits on the ground.

Twice.

After shooting me one last annoyed sort of look, he turns and gapes straight ahead.

Then he does it. I mean, he really does it!

He slaps those long, thin leather reins against Old Stump's backside, makes a kissing sound with his mouth, and takes off—leaving me standing on the dirt road, alone in the dark of the night.

Same way he left my mama the day he stole us away from her!

3

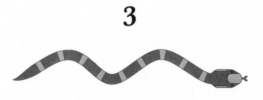

ALONE

Watching the back of that wagon skedaddle down the road, I feel the life being pulled clean out the bottom of my feet. Not a little at a time either, but all of a sudden, the same as if I was being sucked over the side of a mountain by a gigantic waterfall. My stomach's billowing steamy water into my mouth that I've swallowed down so many times my throat's beginning to ache.

I can't believe Daddy left me.

Standing and watching the wagon disappear around the bend, I suddenly realize there's nothing moving around out here. Not a breeze blowing the tree limbs or even a lightning bug moseying by. There's not even any hungry barn owls swooping down and sweeping the meadows in search of a mouse or a rabbit or a lazy evening moth. You can bet your bottom dollar I'm not moving either. Matter of fact I'm not rightly sure I'm even breathing.

Like an extra nose on the face of a warthog, I stand here alone, not sure of the name of the one-horse town we just come from or the one Daddy's got in his mind to go to next. I'm shivering so 'til I'm not sure if my legs will hold me much longer and I can't say if the shivering's from the chill of the night or from my nerves.

For two long years now we've been on the road running to warmer places in winter and cooler ones in the summer, but never, ever in any of my imaginings would I have thought that Daddy would leave me all alone.

What in the world will I do now? Why, my daddy must be out of his mind to go off and leave a young'un—even one he don't much care for—alone in a strange place. And in the dark!

From the silence of it all I reckon the katydids and toads figure the human folk have moved on, because all of a sudden they commence holding a hollering contest from one side of the road to the other. Any other time I would have enjoyed their music; it would have reminded me of Kentucky.

Not now.

Not tonight.

Not when I've got so many of those same conflicting conflicts I had a few hours earlier eating away at the inside of my head.

I don't know how long I stand here, alone, scared, and hungry, with the fierce distaste for my daddy boiling inside of me like a kettle of lye over an open fire. Just as I'm ready to turn and go to walking back the way we come, something in my gut tells me to snatch one last look down the road into the direction my daddy was headed.

Am I seeing right?

Is that what I think it is?

Bending over, looking squinty-eyed into the night, I cock my head from side to side. But when the glimmer from the moon catches the edge of those yellow wheels, it's then that I know for sure. Daddy's stopped that wagon just past the bend of the road and is sitting, waiting for me to catch up.

My shoulders sink, and I'm slouching worse than a one-armed man burdened down with a sack of coal. I sigh. More than anything in the world I want to run down that road and feel the dirt slap my toes through the holes in the bottom of my shoes. I want to jump up into that wagon, grab my daddy around the neck, and thank him for not leaving me. I want to kiss his cheeks and feel his nubby whiskers scratch my face. I want to bury my nose in the collar of his shirt and smell the scent of his sweat mixing with the witch hazel he's slapped onto his neck to heal the cuts from earlier in the day.

But I don't.

I can't. So I do the only thing any other girl in my shoes would do, and that's to take my own sweet time walking that dirt road. After all, I don't want Daddy to think I've got the fear in me, or that I need him.

There's not a turtle anywhere in the South with a dawdle any slower than mine.

When I get to the wagon, it's clear Daddy's no happier with me than he was when he tossed me out onto the road, and he don't mince for words.

"Chestnut, I'm going to say this once, and I don't want to have to ever say it again. Do you understand?"

The madder my daddy gets, the softer he talks, and right at this minute he's practically whispering.

"Yes, sir," I say, my teeth chattering—and not from the cold.

"Your mama's not here and the reason for that doesn't much matter, at least not now you're still a child." He looks me down and back again like he's thinking, or maybe worried he's going to say more than he wants me to hear. "Anyway," he starts in again, "it isn't going to change no matter how bad you or the triplets wish it so. Just give up on all this nonsense of us being together again, you hear? Give it up!"

He shakes his head, swallows hard, and stares out into the night.

"Selling this elixir and traveling from town to town is what we're concentrating on now. It puts food in your stomach and shoes on your feet, however ragged and full of holes them shoes may be. As long as you live with me you'll do what I say, when I say do it, and if that means you have to stretch the truth a bit . . . well . . ." His jaw muscles are jumping up and down so I know he's clenching his teeth. "Well . . . so be it," he says.

Swallowing hard and shivering more than once standing here in the dark of the night, I'm getting fussed at by a man who, even on the best of bad days, I don't much care for. But I don't disrespect him. I make sure my mouth stays closed.

"Chestnut Hill, you're still just a little girl and you don't know what's best. I do. I'm your daddy and I make the decisions for this family. Do you understand?"

"Yes, sir," I mutter, with fists balled so tight I can feel my heartbeat in the tips of my fingers.

"When the trouble started, I told you to stay put inside that wagon. You didn't, and what's more you let your brother out too. You both could have been killed by that mob. What in the world were you thinking, girl?"

I want to holler at the top of my lungs: *I was thinking of you, that's what I was thinking! I was doing my best to try and save your sorry hide from taking a walloping, but I should have let them beat the tarnation plumb out of you.*

But I don't say it. Mama would never take kindly to me sassing Daddy.

"You weren't thinking, were you?"

"No, sir, reckon not."

I shrug and stare at the tops of my dust-covered shoes.

"Well, the next time you go against something I tell you and put yourself and those babies in harm's way, I'll lay a strap to your backside so hard you won't sit for a week. And don't you think for one minute that you're too big for a whooping, you hear?"

He leans over and spits again.

"Yes, sir."

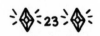

I'm shivering and feeling sicker to my stomach than I've felt in a long time. Daddy's never hit us, but just the threat of a strappin's enough to cause my stomach to do a backwards flip. I don't look at him, but I don't need to. I feel his eyes staring a hole right through me, like he's wishing I was somebody else's child.

"Now," he starts in again, so soft and quiet you'd think there was a newborn baby sleeping in back of that wagon of his. "Get up here, get into bed, and let this be the last we speak of what's happened this evening, you hear? By morning we'll be clean out of this territory with fresh prospects for the elixir and the show."

"Yes, sir."

I glance at him, expecting an offer to help me into the wagon, but instead he holds tight to the reins like he's feared they'll slip from his grip at any second. He stares down the road a piece.

I grab hold to the seat and pull myself up.

The wagon rocks from side to side, and I know it's not my skinny bones doing the rocking. It's those young'uns running away from the door before Daddy sees and swats them back to his way of thinking.

Stepping into the back of the wagon, I slam the door behind me, determined now more than ever to find my mama, get our family back on the straight and narrow, and maybe even take my daddy down a notch or two in the process.

I flop back on my cot, but I'm not ready for sleeping. In the darkness of that wagon, what I'm ready for is thinking.

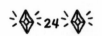

Before I bring myself to think too much though, Filbert commences whispering.

"Chestnut? You all right?"

"Yeah."

"I'm sorry Daddy's mad at you."

"Me too."

"You're a good sister."

"Uh-huh."

Hazel and Mac have already begun to suck in the cool night air in a rhythm that sounds like comfort.

An outraged tear trickles from the corner of my eye, rolling down my face and into my ear. Another one follows and I swipe it with one angry jab, wishing with all of my being I was a hitter. Then again, there's nothing to hit inside an old worn-out circus wagon, so even the thought of it seems useless.

"You thinkin' about Mama?" Filbert asks.

"Yep."

There's a long pause, and then he lets out a long, slow breath.

That's the last we said there in the blackness of the night with only the moon and stars shining through the cracks. But it was only the beginning of my thinking.

Before I can blink more than a half a dozen times, I hear all of them breathing the rhythm of the sleeping.

Not me.

Not when there's so much planning to be done.

4

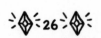

A Puzzlement

I've spent the last two long hot weeks with these babies, packed tighter than Prince Albert in a can in back of this wagon, thinking and planning on putting our family back together. Matter of fact, about all I can do is think while we're bumping along rocky dirt roads, stopping just long enough to build a fire, mix up some food, and let Daddy sleep a wink or two every now and then.

"Filbert, do you ever think about Mama?" I ask, pulling my sketch papers and pencil from under my cot.

"Huh?"

He grunts, not even putting aside his book to look at me.

"Mama. Do you ever think about her and what we'd be doing right now if we were still at home?"

"Nope."

I stare at the top of his head, wishing I could see his face. With Filbert's propensity for stretching the truth, it'd be easier to know if he was being honest if I could look into his eyes.

"I do. I think of her all the time."

"What?" He peers at me from over his picture book, his face all wrinkled and looking perturbed.

"You know, think about Mama and what we'd be doing if we were at home." I sigh and lean back on my cot. "I'd be sitting at that pine table Daddy built, watching Mama cook. I can smell it now: fried chicken, green beans, corn bread. Mmm."

"Mama never cooked that stuff," Hazel says, looking up from her Buster Brown coloring book.

"She cooked all that and more; you were just too young to remember. I'd have my paper and pencils in front of me and I'd be drawing: pictures of her cooking; pictures of Daddy coming home from work all dirty and gritty and sweaty; and pictures of the hills and hollers around the mines."

"Would you draw pictures of me?" Hazel asks.

"No, silly," Mac lisps, slinging his yo-yo straight out, barely missing the side of Hazel's head. "She'd draw a picture of a goat and say it was you! Baaaaah!"

Hazel jumps from the floor, runs over, and slugs Mac on the arm. He drops his yo-yo and draws back a fist.

"Hey! Hey! Hey! You know what Daddy says about fighting, Mac. No hitting girls—ever—for any reason."

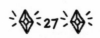

"Chestnut, you're not the boss of me," he yells, letting loose of his fist.

"I like being with Daddy," Filbert says, his eyes turned back to his book. "I'm glad we're not at home. I like being on the road."

"You're just saying that because you're one of Daddy's little pets."

"Well, I'm not his pet and I'm glad we're here with Daddy too," Hazel says.

"Oh sure, he loves and hugs on you, tussles the boys' hair, but he don't hardly even look my way. The way I've got it figured, he don't even like me."

"Chestnut, you take that back!" Hazel shouts, running at me, giving me a shove. "Daddy does too like you, and you know it."

Hazel might still act the part of a baby, but she can pack a punch that'll make you wish you'd brought something to the party besides your fists.

"Does not," I say, shoving her backwards with one easy push.

"Does too."

Another shove.

"I know why Daddy don't like you," Filbert says, tossing his book aside, standing, and stretching like he has the answers to all the world's questions at his fingertips.

I stop the shoving match with Hazel and stare at him. "What do you mean, you know why Daddy don't like me?"

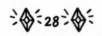

"He told me."

"He told you he didn't like me?"

In less than two giant steps I plant myself toe to toe with Filbert and stare him down.

"Well, he didn't say he didn't like you, exactly."

"What does that mean?" I ask, my heart pounding into my throat and my face getting hotter by the second. I narrow my eyes into a squint and speak through clenched teeth. "You tell me what he said right this minute, Filbert Emanuel Hill, or I'll knock your lights out."

"Okay, okay! But back up. I can't think with you breathing on me like that."

Filbert takes a breath, and there's a sneaky, sly sort of grin that pops out on his face. He must have realized it too because he swipes at his face with his hand.

"All he said was that you remind him of Mama. Since he don't ever talk about her or seem to miss her much, I just figured—"

"Yeah, well you figured wrong!" I interrupt, knocking against him with my stomach.

"Whoa!"

We hear Daddy holler, and the wagon rolls to a stop.

Filbert runs, slings wide the doors, and jumps to the ground, missing the steps completely.

Huh! Good thing he run out before I could get my hands on him.

"Filbert! Mac!" Daddy shouts. "I passed a creek about half a mile back. The two of you take Old Stump and walk

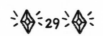

her back. Let her rest a while by the water. There was some high grass there for her too. We'll camp here for now. Hazel, you get the wagon shipshape, and, Chestnut, we could all do with a batch of fresh clothes."

"Where are we now, Daddy?" Mac asks, leaving his yo-yo for the largest earthworm I ever laid eyes to.

"Oh I suspect we crossed over the Tennessee line some time back." Daddy rubs his neck and leans over to touch his toes. "I'd say we're pretty deep in Alabama territory by now."

Mac, not paying any more attention to Daddy's words than our horse, sends the earthworm flying into the trees.

"Quit your stalling now, Mac," Daddy says, "and get on up there and tend to Old Stump."

With Filbert's words still stinging my ears like an angry wasp, I shove the dirty clothes into an empty box and head to the creek behind the boys and the horse. It's not long before I'm slapping wet clothes against the large rocks until my shoulders ache, trying my best to beat the dirt clean out of them. As I scrub and rub them up and down, the stubbornness of that dirt puts me in the mind of Daddy.

Why in the world he run off with us like he did is still such a puzzlement. Every time he opens his mouth and speaks about it he knows he's lying too, but he sticks to his story like a fat tick on the belly of a hound dog.

I know hating is wrong, especially if it's your kin, but thinking about Daddy running off with us like he did sets my

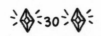

blood to boiling. Reckon a girl would have to try mighty hard not to hate a man for something like that.

My fingers rub and scrub and my mind fusses about Daddy, and before I realize it I've scrubbed the skin clean off my knuckles here against these rocks. There's blood mixing with the icy waters of that fast moving creek too, so much that it shocks me at the sight. If only I could wash Daddy's lies off that easy. But I can't.

Shoving the clean, wet clothes back down into the box, I plop it onto my hip and cart it back to camp where I hang the clothes over tree limbs or lay them flat out on the rocks to dry.

When I get back I see that Daddy's cooking up a pan of taters over the open fire, and the thoughts of a bite or two causes my anger to cool just a bit. After all, with all the room the hunger's taking up in my belly, reckon there ain't as much room for the irritation. With only one panful among us, there's never enough to fill a body to the top, but I don't mind saying that what there is tastes mighty fine.

Before long, late afternoon becomes early evening and the popping and snapping and sparking of the fire begins to feel like contentment—almost as much as the warmth of one of Mama's well-worn quilts in winter. I listen for a while at Daddy's reminiscing over the last two years on the road and all the places we've been in this old wagon. He describes the towns and lets the triplets guess the names and their states.

After a while I tire of their game and pretend not to listen. Instead I stare at the fire and let my mind wander back to home and to Mama. Where is she now? What's she doing and is she missing me as much as I'm missing her?

The wood smoke that's circling draws the late-evening gnats, and when the fireflies light up the sky like flickering candles, the triplets' eyelids begin to droop. When there's more yawns coming from their mouths than words, Daddy says, "Time for bed, young'uns. Tomorrow's a new day full of surprises and possibilities for us and the show."

Following the triplets up the steps and into the wagon, I stop on the top step and give a nod to Mister Moon, the same moon up in the sky that Mama's seeing back in Kentucky. I smile at the thought of it and before I step inside, I whisper, "I love you, Mama. I miss you."

The inside of our old wagon quickly fills with the sounds of the sleeping. With my fingers laced beneath my head, I stare out of the tiny window at the top of the wall into the night sky. I watch the stars twinkle, feel my eyes getting heavy and finally give in to sleep wondering what Daddy meant when he said "Tomorrow's a new day full of surprises."

5

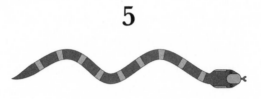

BEING NOSY

"Slim? Slim Hill, dat you?"

It's not a voice easily recognized.

"Abraham?" Daddy shields the morning sun from his eyes with his hand and squints. "Abraham, my friend, goodness, what's it been . . . four, five years now?"

"At least dat, maybe more," the stranger hollers, running toward the wagon to meet Daddy.

The triplets practically fall over the top of each other trying to be the first to get close to the new man in camp. Still not sure of who he is though, I snatch them back and block them from getting any closer. They struggle but it seems like there's more curiosity over who this man is than a desire to break free my hold. They gawk and stare but at least they keep their wonderings to a whisper.

Daddy and the man shake hands and then go to slapping each other on the back like they've known each other for years. They may be friends—now that I look closer he does seem a tad familiar—but the first thing I notice is that Daddy seems to be putting on airs, pretending to be something he's not. Makes me wonder just how close their friendship really is if Daddy has to pretend to be his charming self.

"Come on, let's jaw over a cup of swamp water," Daddy says, motioning Abraham closer to the morning fire.

Keeping out of sight, I try to size him up by his looks. Mama always says you can never be quite sure what's in the can until you pop off its lid, but I've got the good sense to know that you can tell a lot about a person from the feeling you get in your gut the first time you lay eyes to them.

He's a small man, much smaller than Daddy, with short curly hair the color of dandelion fluff. From his looks he's an awful lot like us; he's missed more than a few meals in his lifetime. He's dressed in a striped brown suit, complete with matching vest, tie, and clunky derby hat.

"So, Abraham, how've you been?" Daddy asks, slapping the man on the back again.

"And where in the world are you headed so early in the morning, dressed to the nines like you are?"

Abraham lets out a groan and lowers himself onto a large rock by the fire. "Oh I's been fine," he says. "Since I left de mine, my breathin' much better and I feels like a new man. Doctor say all I need was to get de coal dust out my lungs. Dat stuff will put de healthiest of man in de early grave."

Daddy nods and smiles.

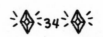

Abraham's talk of the mines jingles my memory like the church bells on a Sunday morning. It's then that I remember him from back home.

"I gots a bit o' business here in town," Abraham says, swigging a sip of coffee. "When did *you* leave de mines?"

"Let's see now, I suppose it was . . ." Daddy scratches his head and looks up at the sky like he's grabbing onto the thoughts of some wise man who's gone on before. "Probably about three and a half, maybe four years now," he says. "Matter of fact it was about six months after you left the mines and moved away that I lost my job. The new owner tried to save a buck or two by cutting back on the number of foremen." Daddy rolls his eyes and rubs at his forehead like he's trying his best to rub away the worry lines.

"No matter though," he adds. "I guess you could say getting away from the mines changed my whole life. I'm not quite sure I can say that it was for the better, but—"

Daddy stops in the middle of a sentence and hangs his head—makes me know in my heart he's thinking about Mama and how he stole us away from her, even though he don't come right out and say it.

"So, what exactly is Slim's Powerful Franciscan Healing Elixir?" Abraham points to the side of the wagon and smiles. From the sly sort of twinkle in his eyes I suspect he's come across some of Daddy's shenanigans before today.

Daddy snickers. "Well now, you know what they say: I could tell you, but if I did I'd have to—"

"I gets it," Abraham says, but I notice right fast that he's not snickering like Daddy. In fact there's a sudden uncomfortable sort of silence between the two of them, and only the sound of coffee being sipped until Abraham starts in again.

"Tell me, Slim, how is dem babies o' yours?"

Daddy tops off his cup with some hot coffee. "This you are not gonna believe," he says. "Chestnut, come on out here. Filbert! Macadamia! Hazelnut! Come in close. I want you all to meet an old friend."

The triplets break my hold and run toward Daddy, circling him like three pesky puppies. I know he called my name too, but still I stay back, near the corner of the wagon.

With his chest puffed out half a mile, Daddy pulls Hazel over in front of him, the buttons of his shirt practically popping with pride. Mama says pride is that feeling that runs up and down your spine right before you fall flat on your face. Once you hit the ground, the only thing left is to pray to die from the embarrassment of it all. From the looks of things I reckon my daddy's fixing to have to pick himself up from the long, hard fall of a lifetime. And then he turns, like he's looking around for me.

When he lays eyes to me he motions me over, but still I stay back, figuring any friend of Daddy's can't be of much use to me. Anyway, if Abraham was really Daddy's friend, Mama would have seen fit to entertain him. She never did.

And since when does Daddy have friends anyway? I've never heard talk of him having any friends.

Still, Daddy nods and smiles, and Filbert and Mac shake Abraham's hand.

"My goo'ness," he says, "dese ain't de triplets is dey? Why, they sho' nuff jes' about growed up. Dey was what, three or so de last time I saw 'em?"

"Believe so," Daddy says, smiling like he's the cat that's choking down the canary. "They're seven now, you know."

"Well they sure is fine-looking childrens, Slim. Yes, sir, dey's fine. Good thing dey don't much looks like you, though."

They laugh, and Daddy nods, but I know in his heart he don't mean it. The way he struts around and works the crowd, I know he thinks he's the finest-looking man this side of the pearly gates. Mama must have thought so too—once upon a time, that is.

Abraham's eyes leave the triplets as he leans around Daddy to lay eyes to me, standing by the edge of the wagon. He smiles. "Dat's not your Chestnut," he says, looking back and forth between me and Daddy.

"Yes. Yes, of course it is. Come on over here, baby. It's all right, don't mind Abraham. He's known of you children since you were born. Don't you remember seeing him around the mines?"

I shrug, but seeing him up close seals my recollection of him now. Daddy used to walk into and out of the mines with a Negro man every day. Reckon from what Daddy's saying, that man must have been Mister Abraham.

Abraham stands, and removes his hat.

I hang my head and stare at my shoes.

"Oh, Slim, she be de spittin' image o' her mama. So perty, and all growed up," he says, still looking back and forth between Daddy and me.

I turn to walk away but not before I notice that suddenly Abraham's not smiling.

"Speakin' of your wife . . ." He clears his throat and turns back to the fire, looking like he might be searching for words. "Slim," he asks, in a voice suddenly low and serious. "Jes' where is your Mavis?"

6

Mind Your Beeswax

Daddy ignores Abraham's question and soon their morning talk spills over into late afternoon, but even Daddy can't stop the questions forever with a simple changing of the subject. Abraham asks Daddy again, and this time he looks around us young'uns like he's waiting for Mama to pop out from the wagon after hearing her name another time or two.

Daddy, his face as washed-out as the morning ashes after a late night's fire, doesn't say a word. He just shakes his head, and for the first time in as long as I can remember I feel a might . . . well, I reckon you could say I feel a might sorry for my daddy. Reckon it pains him something fierce to have to tell an old friend he's snatched us up and run off with us without Mama knowing about it.

No way I'm leaving now, so I just sit tight and hold on fast to the smooth log beneath me.

Maybe, just maybe, for once I'll learn the why of it all. Mama always says if you want to learn the facts about something, keep your mouth shut and your ears open. She says the Good Lord gave us two ears and one mouth for one reason: so's we could listen twice as much as we say. Right at this minute my mouth is closed so tight even the tiniest of gnats couldn't make its way past my lips, and my ears are peeled back and listening sharper than a mountain lion with an empty belly.

Daddy clears his throat, then pokes a stick into the fire and stirs it until the sparks dance and disappear into the low-hanging branches of the trees, the smells of wood smoke and bitter coffee hanging low and circling around the camp.

I fold my arms across my chest and strain to hear Daddy and Abraham's conversation above the triplets' whoops and hollers as they play a rough and tumble game of chase around the wagon. Patting my foot against the dry, packed dirt, I stare into the fire wishing I had the paints and the time and the smarts to put this scene to canvas; me with all the hot cayenne reds of my anger toward Daddy, him with the buttery yellow of his cowardness from stealing us away mixed in with the stormy-water blues of his embarrassment over Mama not being around when his old friend asks about her. And then there's Abraham. I've not yet come up with the colors to describe Daddy's friend, so for now I'd just paint him as neutral, like the stringy, eggy-white cobwebs of a dewy morning or the tans of the turtle doves that coo on top of the fence posts as Old Stump clips along at a slow, got-no-where-to-go sort of pace.

But the truth of it all is that I can't wait to hear the tale Daddy's going to tell. Seeing as how he's an expert at lying, I just know this one's going to be a doozy!

"Chestnut," he says, "why don't you take the others inside and work on their . . ."

Mama says interrupting adult conversations is bad manners and something a proper Southern lady would never do, but I reckon if I don't make an exception just this once, Daddy'll hem and haw and search for words until the evening sun puts itself to bed. After all, that's what liars do isn't it? Stumble and stammer around for words?

"Reading," I say, my arms folded and brow worked into a wrinkle. "You want me to work on their reading?"

"Yes. Reading. That's good."

Daddy's forehead is wrinkled and scrunched up like he's puzzled or nervous. He lets out a long sigh like he's relieved I come up with the right words.

Huh! Saved his sorry hide is what I've done, and he knows it same as me.

I turn and stare a hole right through him as I steer the triplets up the steps and into the wagon.

"Chestnut's not only their big sister, Abraham, but she's been their teacher these last two years that we've been on the road, taking what she's learned from her schooling and seeing to it that the babies are learned in proper. She's taught them to read and got them ready for school—when the time comes for us to settle down that is," Daddy says.

"Go on inside," I say to the triplets, maybe a little proud but even more surprised that Daddy would say a good word about me to a friend. To my way of thinking though it's gonna take more than one good word to get him out of the fix he's in with me.

"Pull out your reading books and I'll be along in a minute," I say, but I've got no intention of going inside. Not without some answers to my wonderings.

I stop, halfway up the steps and wait, barely taking in air. I've got the good sense to know this man's going to talk about my mama, and I want to be around to hear every word he has to say. I move as far back on the steps as I can, so as not to be seen by either of them.

"Now den, you jes' tell ol' Abraham about yo' wife, Slim. Where in de world is she at?"

I know Daddy well enough to know his head is probably hung low, maybe even between his knees. He's rubbing it with his hand and probably spitting on the ground a time or two. He doesn't say a word for the longest time and there's such an uncomfortable silence hanging low, it makes the chilly bumps stand up like soldiers on my arms. Quiet as a church mouse at an all-day dinner, I lean over and try to peek at the two of them.

Abraham starts in again, and I push myself back up against the wagon. "What happened, Slim? It ain't like you

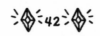

to be here wit'out Mavis. And I gots to tell you, a man alone with four young childrens? Well . . . it jes' don't looks right."

Daddy clears his throat, and I hear him pouring another cup of coffee.

"You and Mrs. Mavis was happy. Least dat's what you always say and de way it look to de outsiders." He lays a hand on Daddy's shoulder. "Now come on, Slim. You can tell ol' Abraham. What be going on?"

Drinking in every word, I breathe slow and shallow, knowing there are secrets that Daddy hasn't told me. Maybe this Abraham knows the truth, but if he don't, I reckon Daddy's fixing to tell him.

"Yeah, well things aren't always as they seem, are they, Abraham?" Daddy asks. "We had that real once-upon-a-time kind of love once, but, well, she run off and left me a couple of years ago."

I stretch and lean out a little, just enough so's I can peek at them out of one eye.

Abraham doesn't look surprised at Daddy's tale at all. "Well den, I reckons dat was hard on you, Slim, you bein' an orphan yo'self and all. Dat woman was de only real family you had, 'cept de childrens o' course."

Daddy sighs a relaxing, after-a-hot-bath sort of sigh. "You have no idea, Abraham. I mean when she said she wouldn't be back until I could put her and the young'uns in a respectable home, I don't mind telling you, I was stunned. I mean, she left me holding the bag with—"

43

"You bes' stop dere, Slim," Abraham interrupts. "Now, we not seen each other since I left de mines, but we know each others a long, long time. Don't you think I deserve de truth?"

I'm listening—straining to hear—but Daddy don't oblige.

After the longest bit of silence I ever did hear, Abraham starts in again.

"Slim," he says, "I'm gon' tell you now dat I saw your Mavis a while back, but she tol' me a different story, so don't go puttin' on airs for me."

I swallow down a gasp. All of a sudden, more questions than answers run around in my head. Was Mama here, or did he see her somewhere else? How did she look? Did she say anything about us? Was she looking for us?

I knew it!

There's more to this story than Daddy's telling, and this man knows what it is. Now I'm going to finally find out the whole story, and when I do—

"Wait a minute, Abraham," Daddy whispers. "You know what they say: little pitchers have big ears; and the way your gums are flapping you're liable to fill up every pitcher within miles around."

Daddy clears his throat and yells out, "Chestnut Hill?"

Now how in the world from where he's sitting with his back to the wagon does he know I'm here? I'm being as quiet as a sleepy fly on a church bench, barely sucking in air at all. Just for a second I think about not answering Daddy, but reckon he never has taken kindly to being ignored. "Yes, sir?" I say, sort of timid and quiet.

"You go on now and do as I say. Shut that door and help your brothers and sister with their reading."

"Yes, sir."

I stomp up the steps a-fierce mad at my daddy and aiming to be sure that he knows it.

"What's happening?" Filbert asks when I open the door and then slam it—hard—behind me. "What are they talking about?"

"Sssh!"

I run through the wagon, then open wide the front door as quiet as I can. I ease out onto the bench where Daddy rides behind Old Stump, hold my breath, and listen, but all I can make out are the low rumbles of men talking. I stretch and lean over, trying my best to get closer to hear their words; still, I can't make them out. But I've just got to know about my mama. I have to know the story—the whole story—and I'm aiming to find out if it's the last thing I do.

Holding to the side of the wagon, I bend as far out as I can. Standing up on tiptoe, I stretch and reach and lean, and before I know what's happening, I'm flying out of that wagon, smacking the dirt facedown, sprawled out flatter than a busted egg on the ground right in front of Abraham and my daddy.

7

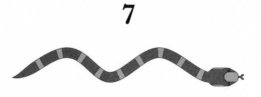

Lost Coins

Daddy jumps to his feet.

"Chestnut, what in the world are you doing?"

He steps over Abraham and reaches a hand down to pull me to my feet.

"Um, well . . . uh, I just—" Now I'm on the other end of the hemming and hawing, stumbling and stammering around, searching for words, and let me tell you it's every bit as unpleasant as it sounds.

I rub the dust from my face, slap it from my dress, and brush my knees with my hands. They're stinging and burning from the fall, and I'm pretty sure at least one of them is bleeding, but I'm not dare going to bend over and look.

"Uh-huh, that's what I thought," Daddy said. "Your ears are bigger than your brain. You're messing around in business you've got no cause to be messing around in, and making a fool of yourself to boot. Now get on up in that wagon and stop all this nonsense. Don't let me have to tell you again, you hear?"

"Yes, sir."

Reluctantly, I go back in the same way I come out, but I'm not happy. I didn't hear one lick of what Abraham and Daddy were saying about my mama. Makes me mad, but I won't give up. No sir, I'll find out the truth if it's the last thing I do.

Seems like hours that Abraham and Daddy continue talking and I'm left inside with them three young'uns, working on reading—reading, of all things.

I'm tired and can't remember when I've been so happy to see the night lights peeking through the windows at the top of the wagon's wall. I reckon Abraham and Daddy must have talked until way up in the night because I drifted off to sleep listening to the low mumbling tones of their voices.

Sometime in the night though I feel the bump, bump, bumping of the wagon wheels and I know by that we're headed to another town, maybe even another state. Reckon most girls my age would be happy to travel around and see the country. Not me. I won't let myself be happy until I find my mama and put our family back together.

I open my eyes and stare through the window with so many thoughts running around in my head that there's no way I could possibly turn off my brain enough to get back to sleep. Where's Abraham, and what did he say about my mama? What's made Daddy leave town so fast? We didn't even do a show and it's not like Daddy to miss a chance at making money.

After the longest night I can remember, the morning sun don't have a chance to wake me. Daddy pounds on the side of the wagon yelling, "Get up, sleepyhead!"

Mercy, that man can work a nerve.

"Come on, Chestnut," Daddy yells. "We're heading into town for supplies. We'll leave the wagon here for now."

I smooth my dress with my hands and slip my shoes on my feet, but not before reaching way back under my cot and sliding out my metal box, taking out what I've saved and shoving it into my pocket.

I climb on out and eye the triplets. "Where's that Abraham man?" Mac asks, flipping his yo-yo out and back again.

"Never mind," Daddy says, making sure Old Stump's reins are tied to a tree close to the wagon. He gives her rump a friendly sort of smack and picks her feet up to look at her shoes. "Abraham's got his own things to tend to."

With coins jingling in my pocket like a handful of rusty skeleton keys, I'm following Daddy and the triplets into town, studying the houses that dot the grassy hills as few and far between as the freckles across the nose of a hound dog. It all puts me in the mind of the poorer folks' homes back in Kentucky. Then again, I reckon there's poor folk everywhere, even in towns with fancy names and buildings that reach up and touch the sky like this Birmingham.

Filbert and Mac run up ahead, but Hazel is holding tight to Daddy's hand and looking up at him all googly-eyed. She cuddles his hand, kisses and swings it back and forth, and smiles and jumps along beside him like a toddler chasing after an all-day sucker.

Hazel—all show and no substance, prancing around like the world revolves around her—just like Daddy. Cut from the same piece of cloth, them two are.

"Chestnut gots money," she says.

"She does?" Daddy asks, pretending to act surprised. Dressed in a pair of his black show pants and a white shirt, it reminds me of how he dressed back home on Sundays, when we'd walk to church as a family.

"And just how much money does Chestnut have, and where, pray tell, did she get it?"

He looks down at Hazel then looks back over his shoulder at me and winks. I can tell that he doesn't believe her, and by the tone of his voice he's just going along with her for fun.

"She gots twenty dollars."

"Not dollars, Hazel, cents; twenty-eight cents to be exact, and I found it, thank you very much." Mercy. That girl works my nerves.

Daddy stops walking and turns to face me, like he's suddenly run into a brick wall.

"So, where did you get the money?" he asks, the smile on his face fading.

"I found it," I say, and I don't say it nice either. I even catch myself smirking before I realize what I'm doing.

He cocks his head sideways, like a dog trying to figure out people talk. By the look on his face he's asking for more of an explanation, so I reckon it's up to me to give it.

I want to smart off, knowing that his not trusting me is at the heart of his question, but I don't. Matter of fact, I practice his tactic for a change, and take a deep breath before I speak. Then I let the words that come out of my mouth be just as quiet as I can—but so's he can still hear them of course.

"Everywhere we go," I say, "I look for coins along the streets and gullies. Folks lose them and I find them. I pick them up, put them in my pocket, and save them."

"Oh?"

He shoots me a look that makes me feel less than twelve again—a look that says he don't believe me.

I hang my head. "Yes, sir," I say, shoving my hand as far down in my pocket as I can, grabbing hold to my change, and scrubbing the toe of my shoe across the dry dust of the gravel-strewn road. Dirt and tiny pebbles squeeze in through the holes in the bottoms of my shoes, working their way between my toes.

"So, what are you planning to do with all that money?" he asks.

"I'm not rightly sure," I say, still staring at the ground but knowing all the while the plan I've conjured up.

There's no way I'm going to tell him my plan though. No way he would understand.

So, I lie—just like he's taught me to do.

I shrug and scuff a shallow trench in the dirt with my shoe. "I might just keep on saving it, or I might see something in the store that I want."

The words come out easy—more easy than they should for them to be a lie—but it's the sinking, sick-like, you-done-something-bad sort of feeling that comes after the words that feels the worst.

All he says is "Humph," and then he turns his back to me. He cradles Hazel's hand and off we go, just the same as if we'd never had a conversation at all.

I sigh, but I'm sort of proud that I didn't jump back and yell at him like he expected, realizing too that if he knew what I was planning, he'd tan my hide just for thinking it.

The closer we get to town, the better things start to smell, like fried chicken and fresh baked bread. There's a sweetness in the air too, like the scent from pies or cakes or cookies pulled fresh from the oven. It all reminds me of Sunday dinners with Mama.

"Why so quiet, Chestnut?" Daddy asks after a while of listening to the triplets' shouts and hollerings.

"No reason," I say as we head down the street alongside other folks we don't yet know. "Just thinking."

We walk under a metal sign near the train station that's so tall it nearly touches the sky. It reads:

BIRMINGHAM, THE MAGIC CITY!

Birmingham's streets are wide and made of bricks lined side by side. There are large metal streetcars running right through the middle of town, their tiny wheels sinking deep into the little grooves cut and buried in the bricks.

There are the biggest buildings I've ever seen, some of them as wide as they are tall, with names right on the front of them in huge white letters. There's nothing like this back in the hills and hollers of Kentucky, that's for sure.

Across from the theater—The Alabama—and next to The Alabama Bank, in the middle of town is a large store with a skinny sign high on the side of the building that reads DRY GOODS GENERAL STORE.

Mac and Filbert see it first and make their presence known to the folks inside by cupping their hands around their eyes and peering in through the big glass window in front.

The doors of the store swing wide and pine boards line the floor from front to back. Never in my life have I seen floors so polished and shiny. Why, you could almost see your reflection, if you was to get down on your knees and look close enough, that is.

Shelves that stretch from floor to ceiling line the walls and are planted down the middle of the store too. From the looks of things, there's everything on those shelves you could ever dream of having or wanting.

The triplets' mouths are hung open down to their chests and their necks stretched back about as far as a neck can go. For the first time in a long while Hazel's been empty of words and I don't mind saying, it don't bother me in the least.

I stay back as usual, away from Daddy and the triplets, but close enough to see them from the corner of my eye.

The young'uns are touching and handling and picking up everything in sight, and it makes me as nervous as a baby rabbit in a bear cave thinking they're going to grab up something important and shatter it into pieces.

You'd think they'd never been in a store before.

Then again, reckon a big old store like this, they haven't.

All of a sudden I hear a loud crashing sound. I whirl around expecting to look right into the eyes of one of the boys.

But I don't.

It's Hazel's eyes that are filled with tears and her face is as white as a cotton ball.

8

BROKEN DISHES AND WIGGLY BELLIES

I didn't do it! I promise! My hands were in my pockets the whole time," Hazel wails.

And as if I didn't know what was coming next, she covers her face with her hands and goes to sobbing. Weeping, wailing sobs.

I stare at her, afraid to breathe, much less move.

A lady dressed to the nines in a red suit and large ivory hat covered in red flowers steps up. "The little one's right," she says. "It was me. My purse rubbed against the platter and I'm afraid I've dragged it from the counter in my haste. I'll be happy to pay."

Never in all my days have I been so happy to see a fancy, big-hatted lady in the middle of a confession.

I run to Hazel and pull her to me, patting her back while she sobs.

"Hear that, Hazel? You didn't do a thing. This nice lady says it was her purse that done it."

I sigh, letting out the deep breath I didn't realize I'd been holding.

"Uh-huh," Hazel sobs.

I look around for Daddy, but as usual he's nowhere to be found when he's needed.

I raise Hazel's chin with my hand and wipe her tears with the heel of my hand.

"You okay now?" I ask.

She nods.

I leave her side with my eyes jumping from wall to wall and on everything in between. This is one of the biggest stores I've ever been in, and I'm not aiming to miss a thing.

Stacked to the brim with everything from flour to fabric, from cornmeal to candy, and from canning jars to coffee cups, all shiny, bright, and new, them shelves seem to have it all, but what I'm looking for I don't see at first glance.

"Excuse me, sir," I say to the man behind the counter with the wide red mustache, all curled and swirled and circled on the ends. "Do you have any paper?"

"What kind of paper, little missy?" he asks in a voice so booming and loud it could wake the lions in the jungle from right here in downtown Birmingham. "Newspaper, cigarette paper, wrapping paper, toilet—"

I shake my head real fast, like a cat slinging milk from its whiskers.

"No, sir," I interrupt. "What I need is going-to-school type of paper. The kind you practice writing letters and numbers on."

"Oh, you want loose-leaf paper. It's back here," he says, pointing toward the back of the store.

His belly moves from behind the counter before the rest of him, and it jiggles up and down with each step that he takes. He's limping, like he has a game leg, and from behind, where I am, it's clear that one of his shoes is large and clunky and bigger than the other. He limps down the aisle between the door and the shelves toward the back of the store.

I tag along as close behind as I can.

Along the way we pass two closed doors with a sign above that reads:

RESTROOMS

WHITE   COLORED

"What's that?" I ask, pointing to the doors with the signs.

He stops and whips around so fast I have to put my hands up to keep from running into the back of him.

"What do you mean '*What's that*,' child? Haven't you ever seen indoor toilets?"

"I have, sir, but——"

He narrows his eyes, and his one long eyebrow dips low in the middle of his forehead. "Well then, what's the problem? You know about keeping whites and Negros apart, don't you?"

I shake my head, wondering why in the world anyone would want to keep the two apart.

"What sort of backwoods country folk are you anyway, missy?"

He slicks back his circus-red hair with his fingers and gapes at me like he's wondering if the likes of me even ought to be setting foot in a proper store like his.

I don't say anything, but his question starts me to thinking back to what used to be my home. Daddy and Abraham—I know it was now—went down into that big old hole in the earth every day of the week. Except Sunday of course. Funny thing though, in the morning, Abraham looked different than Daddy because of his dark skin. But when Daddy and Mister Abraham came out of the mines in the evening, both of them all black and covered head to toe with coal dust, they both looked the same.

The way I see it, I might be country folk like the mustache man says, but even us backwoods bumpkin country folk got the good sense to know Negros is just the same as white folk, except for the skin on the outside. And the way I got it figured, neither of us—whites or Negros—have got much say in the matter.

About the time I'm doing my wondering, staring right hard at them signs above the doors, a Negro lady with her arms stuffed with packages steps from behind the one marked COLORED.

I grab the door and pull it open wider, so she can come on out without knocking the fire out of her elbows or tripping over her feet that she can't see because of the bundles.

The lady smiles and gives me a wink and a nod, mouths the words "Thank you," and hurries through the store and on her way.

The man with the curly mustache and wiggly belly turns and shoots me a look, like he wants to ask if I understand now that I've seen it with my own eyes. But he don't.

Good thing too, because I'd be asking him what in the world all the hubbub is all about anyhow. Seems to me I remember the preacher back home saying the ground was level at the foot of the cross. Reckon that applies to crotchety store owners with big clunky shoes same as it does to friendly Negro ladies with arms full of packages, now don't it? Way I see it that even puts us backwoods country folk on the same ground with the both of them.

"You got money to pay?" he bellows, jerking my mind away from the writing above the doors and the lady with the smiling face and armload of packages.

"Yes, sir," I say, tapping my hand against my pocket so he can hear the jingling of the coins.

He looks me up and down again and shakes his head.

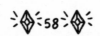

"Is this what you're looking for?"

He shoves the pack of paper up under my nose and I nod. Scowling, he lets go of the paper.

"Well, yes, sir," I say, looking at it more closely, "but don't you have some without the lines, like for drawing pictures and the like?"

"Oh, drawing paper. Well why didn't you say that the first time? It's over here."

He stretches and reaches to the top shelf and pulls down a pack of white drawing paper. He holds it up and shows me, raising one bushy eyebrow like he wants to ask if I'm satisfied now, but he don't.

"Yes, sir, that's it. Thank you."

He turns to walk off.

"Sir? How much is it? I mean, how much does it cost?"

"One hundred sheets for a nickel," he says. He starts walking away and goes to limping fast, like he's in a hurry and can't be bothered with the likes of backwoods country folk like me.

"Oh, and, sir?"

He stops in his tracks but don't even look at me this time.

"Where are your pencils and crayons, please?"

He points to a table at the far end of one of the long lines of shelves, close to the front. "Crayons, eight for a nickel, pencils, a few cents more," he growls. "*Kids,*" I hear him say to the man standing close. "I'm trying to run a business here. What I don't have time for are kids and their questions."

I shove the paper up under my arm and take off behind him to the front of the store, having to run a few steps in order to catch up, and snatching a pack of sharpened pencils and a green and gold box of Crayola crayons as we get close. I'm aiming to give him my money before Daddy sees and asks why I need so much paper. If he finds out and asks about my plans, he won't think twice about tanning my backside with a strap.

I pull the money from my pocket and slap it on the counter lickety-split, my hands sweaty and mouth as dry as a cotton ball in a windstorm. From the back of the store Daddy peers up front and catches my eye.

There's no doubt about it, I've been caught.

"Would you put the paper and pencils into a sack for me, please?" I ask, fearing my plan to get out of the store fast is about to be squashed.

9

THE BLACK BOOK KNOWS THE TRUTH

Before Daddy makes his way to the front of the store, I point to the front doors and mouth the words "I'll be outside."

He nods and smiles, and I reckon—for now at least—I've got away with the first part of my plan, paying for the paper and the pencils and crayons.

I can't wait to get back to the wagon and set it all into motion.

I open the door, and just as I set one foot outside, I feel Hazel slip her hand into mine, following me through the tall double glass doors. We lean against the large picture window, waiting on Daddy and the boys.

Just as I figured, it's not long before Hazel breaks into questions.

"Whatcha got in that sack?" she asks, letting loose my hand and standing on her tiptoes.

"Paper, pencils, and crayons."

"Whatcha gonna do with them?" Her eyes are dancing like a ballerina twirling on a fancy music box.

"Draw." I turn my back to her.

"Can I draw too?" She pulls at my sleeve.

"No." I shove the sack up under my arm and cross my arms over my chest.

She pulls my sleeve again, and I glance over my shoulder at her. Giving me the most pitiful puppy dog look I've ever seen, she pokes out her bottom lip, then suddenly crosses her eyes and sticks out her tongue.

I can't help but laugh.

"I need all of this paper, Hazel. Maybe next time, all right?"

For now she's hushed, and before long Daddy and the boys come from the store with more than any of them can carry. I take one of the boys' bags and hide my sack inside it so Daddy doesn't ask questions. We head back to the wagon and then we wait.

As a matter of fact, we wait three days, more time in one place than we've been in a while. I'm not sure exactly what we're waiting for either. It don't seem from his actions like Daddy's in a hurry to do a show here.

At breakfast, Daddy begins the day by making an announcement.

"I'm going into town alone today. Chestnut, you watch out after the babies."

"Can I come?" Hazel asks.

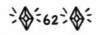

"No. I need to go alone. I've got errands to run and I need to get my jacket repaired for the next show. I won't be long." And off he goes into town with his torn jacket slung over his arm and not so much as a glance back at us.

I'm glad he's gone. Now that I've got the paper and pencils I needed, I can work on my plan to get back to Mama. I don't want him to see me drawing, but I do realize now that if Daddy'd seen, he'd probably have thought this paper was for teaching the young'uns, so maybe I didn't need to hide it so carefully.

Sometimes I miss school—all of the questioning and the smell and feel of the books. Reckon though I've got more schooling in my head than some kids back home will ever have. Most of the kids I knew had to quit school to help their family around the farms. But I still miss it. For two years all I've had to keep the learning fresh in my brain are the books Daddy's picked up along the way in yard sales and even in the missionary's ragbags. But those books aren't mine. I have to use them to teach the babies.

Sometimes I want to tell Daddy how I feel. But before I get the chance he's spouting out words saying there's more to learning than what happens in the classroom. He says knowing how to get along with people is just as important as listening to a teacher recite facts all day long.

Pretty words. Fancy words, but the way I see it he's just making excuses to keep from going back home where we ought to be.

"Stay close and don't go running off," I holler to the triplets as I take the wagon steps two by two and skedaddle inside to work. I can hear them outside, running, playing hide-n-seek and chase, so for now at least, I know all is well.

Searching through Daddy's bag of personal things, I find his little black book where he writes down important stuff like how many bottles of elixir we sell, how much money we make, and which town we're going to next. He makes sure he keeps his black book hid from us so I know I'd better work fast.

In the afternoon, by the time Daddy gets back, I've drawn up twenty flyers, complete with a picture of our wagon and the name of Daddy's elixir on the side. Beneath the wagon, in big clear letters, I've added the final important touch: **Heading to New Orleans, Louisiana!** Looks pretty good too, if I do say so myself.

I'm aiming to nail them to every post in town, right before the wagon pulls out and before Daddy figures out what I've done. If Mama's looking for us same as I'm looking for her, she won't have to hunt. From now on before we leave every town, I'm aiming to nail up flyers notifying her of where we'll be next. You can bet your bottom dollar I'll do my part to help her track us down.

The way I've got it figured I'm as good as home and wrapped up safe in Mama's loving arms!

10

Showtime!

"Come on, Chestnut! You're being a procrastinator. The day's a-wastin'," Daddy yells, smacking his fist against the side of the wagon. "Folks are gathering in town and we're on the move. Time to look alive, girl!"

We're usually up before the dawn, but for once I've had the pleasure of sleeping late. I rub the night grit from my eyes and swing wide the tall wooden wagon doors, staring straight into the thinning spot on the back of Daddy's head, the morning sun shining on it like a spotlight. Mercy, he really ought to wear a hat, and somebody should tell him.

It won't be me.

I gather the triplets—already up and playing like cowboys—into the back of the wagon and straighten their clothes for the show as best as I can.

Lingering aromas of burnt wood and charred iron skillets sunk deep into the leftover bonfire hang low, circling the camp and practically starving me to death. Daddy jumps onto the wagon and guides Old Stump slowly away from camp and down the road into town.

What I wouldn't give for just one more bowl of last night's yellow-eyed beans. The triplets need it more than me though. After all, they've not got their growth yet, and I do. Still, just once I'd love to have all I can eat of something. Anything.

Once we're in the heart of town, Daddy hops from the wagon and weaves like a bobwhite in an open field, trying his best to see if anyone's watching. He hops back up on the seat behind Old Stump, opens the door, and leans in cautiously.

"Be careful now, Chestnut," he says. "Folks across the street are stirring. Don't let them see you. Remember to swing to the back of the wagon before you jump off."

It's been more than three years now since Daddy lost his job and conjured up his get-rich-quick scheme. And in the two years we've been on the road I'll bet I've heard his "Be careful now, Chestnut" speech at least a million times.

He meets me around back, already dressed for the show.

"Tie my tie, Chestnut, baby. My hands are shaking worse than a newborn calf in a hail storm."

I reach up and take the stiff black strings of his new tie between my fingers and begin shaping them into a bow. After two years of this you'd think he'd have his nerves under control.

He looks me in the eyes and smiles, but I look away fast and swallow hard. Just for a second I think maybe he's not so bad. And then he has to go and ruin the moment.

"Baby, you're so pretty," he says. "Why, you know, Abraham was right. You are the spitting image of your mama. I'll bet you look just like she did when she was twelve."

I don't look at him.

I can't.

If I do, I might start to care about him more than I want.

Anyway, I've still got Filbert's words about how Daddy don't like me because I look like Mama still knocking away at my brain.

After a bit Daddy starts in again, but this time he don't finish.

"With that dark-as-night black hair and them big chestnut-brown eyes . . ." His words trail off and he rubs my cheek sort of gentle-like. "Those freckles that jump across your nose just like hers. Aw, she was a looker all right."

It's right then that it happens, same as always. His mind changes gears just as fast as if a conductor had flipped a switch at a railroad junction, as if a train was headed down one path and suddenly was flung onto another. With his "You're so pretty," and "Chestnut, tie my tie," then all of a sudden he flips his own switch and goes off in another direction. His face loses all expression. His smile's gone and the tone of his voice suddenly cross. He looks way off like he's recalling some past memory he don't want me to know anything about.

"But I suppose I can't get my mind on her now, can I?" He shakes his head fast. "No use crying over spilt milk, right?"

Oh, I know what he's doing. He's getting mad, letting bad memories work him up for the show. There's a look in his eyes that's suddenly wild and unruly, like an animal pacing in a cage.

"She's made her bed," he says, shoving a balled fist into the air. "Let her lie in it!"

He beats his fist against the wagon a couple times more, breathes in deep, and then clears his throat. "Who needs her anyway?" he says. "I've got all the happiness I need here on the road raising my little nut farm, alone."

He's sweating. He always sweats before a show—even if the air is cool, like it is today. He says it's his nerves, and that what he needs is a long, slow draw from a big imported cigar.

Huh! Now how could he afford something like that?

He sets his black top hat—the one he bought off a magician over in Knox County—onto his head, slips on his long black coat, and turns to go, looking more like a funeral director or even a preacher than an elixir salesman.

When he reaches the edge of the wagon, he turns back to face me. With a strange, uncommon tenderness in his voice all over again, he says it—same as always, "Chestnut, your mama's leaving was a bad thing, but she left because of me, on account of I couldn't settle down and put her in a good home. You believe me now, don't you?"

Knowing his words by heart, I nod, but I don't believe it no more now than I did the first time he said them. Not deep down inside anyway—where it really counts. I know there's

more to the story than what he's telling, especially since his words don't match up with my recollection.

He flashes me a half smile, straightens his jacket, and sucks in a slow, deep breath. He pats himself on the stomach, rocks up on his tiptoes and back down again a couple of times, like he's revving up a tractor, and off he goes to the front of the wagon, smiling like a Cheshire cat.

The triplets streak past, caught up in a feisty game of chase.

"Whoa! Whoa! Whoa!"

I reach out and grab hold of Hazel by the dress-tail. Filbert and Mac run one more time around the wagon before coming to a stop.

"Come on now, you three. Calm down. It's almost time for the show."

Reaching way down, I brush the mud off Filbert's pants. It's clear to see he spent his morning wading the creek. That boy don't obey worth a lick. If I know him, he's shoved a frog in one pocket and a lizard in the other. Reckon they'll jump out any second now and scare the life plumb out of me, even though I'm halfway expecting it to happen.

I spit in my hand and do my best to smooth the cowlick in the front of Mac's hair, but he jerks away before it's done. Poor Mac. What God gave him in face value, He took away when it comes to his bottlebrush hair.

I give my thumb a lick and then wipe a smudge from Hazel's chin. Mercy, somebody ought to follow this girl around with a rag. She just can't stay clean. I brush the dust from her dress the best I can, but it's not easy, especially since she's wiggling worse than an earthworm in a rainstorm.

A sudden sputtering causes the three of them to turn and stare with their mouths hung open to their chests. It's a shiny black Model T, sputtering and coughing down the street like a cat hocking up a windpipe full of mouse whiskers.

"What are you gawking at? You've seen cars before."

"Yeah," says Mac, pointing, "but not ones making that kind of racket. Something's wrong with that one!"

His words start my mind to thinking. Here we are in the middle of 1921, just about two and a half years from the end of the big World War, the boys home from fighting and driving around in their fancy Model Ts. Then there's us, stuck in the olden days, still riding around in a rickety old wooden wagon. And we wonder why folks call us "backwoods."

Now don't get me wrong. As wagons go, ours is a fine one, even though it did used to be a circus wagon. Daddy says they kept animals right where we're sleeping now. Sometimes I lie awake at night and listen for the ghosts of old lions and tigers—maybe even bears—and wonder what they must have thought of their wagon ride.

Then there's Old Stump, our mare. Bless her heart. Mama always says you can say anything you want about a body—good or ill—as long as you put "bless their heart" right along with it. Sort of takes away the hurt of it all, I suppose.

Anyway, Daddy traded a man our old worn-out horse and ten bottles of elixir for her when we spent a few days over in Memphis. I'd have to think mighty long and hard to know who got the worst end of that deal or why Daddy would trade one exhausted horse for another.

Old Stump's lost all the hair off her backside, one of her ears is longer than the other, but she's as dependable as the day is long. She's a-fierce tired out of her eyes too, but then why wouldn't she be, dragging us and our big old wooden wagon in and out of practically every town in the South for the last two years and more?

"Look alive, now! Look alive!" Daddy yells.

"All right," I whisper, bending down and looking the triplets in the eyes. "You know how Daddy gets before a show. Be on your best behavior, please."

"Chestnut, you're not the boss of us," Mac says, propping his hands on his hips, his lisp cutting the air.

"You're our sister, not our mama!" Hazel says, sticking out her tongue and sucking it back in again.

"Come around here, young'uns," Daddy says, calling the triplets to the front of the wagon.

"Filbert," I hear him say, "you take the melody. Mac and Hazel, you do harmony this time."

"Aw, Daddy," Hazel whines. "I'm sick of singing harmony. Why can't I do the melody and let the boys do the harmony?"

I peek around the corner and see Filbert, wagging his finger in Hazel's face, but not where Daddy can see. I reckon he's just a tad too smart for that. His head wobbles from side to side as he mouths the words "'Cause I said so, that's why," just before those same words come spewing from Daddy's mouth.

Hazel smacks Filbert on the back.

Hard.

Good thing for her Daddy don't allow the boys hitting on us girls or she'd be road dirt by now.

I'm leaning against the wagon trying to fix my own hair by running my fingers through it when Daddy yells, "It's all about the show young'uns; it's all about the show."

But it's not.

With him, it's all about the money.

"All right now," he says. "Showtime! Chestnut, make your move!"

11

GRANNY TALES

I amble from the wagon, trying my best to look like I belong to this fancy, citified town—but how could I? Dress two sizes too big and shoes with holes all in them. How could I look like I belong anywhere but backwoods Kentucky? Reckon the mustache man was right.

I tag along close behind some folks holding tight to young'uns of their own.

"Why, hello there!" Daddy hollers, motioning the few people stirring 'round in the streets over with a wave of his hand. "You folks look a bit tired, sort of run down and ailing. Looks like you could use a pick-me-up! C'mon and step right up close to the wagon here. I've got just the thing you need."

It's not long before the crowd grows. Seems folks always go to congregating when there's a commotion about, and Daddy makes sure he works up a commotion. The more folks that come around, the louder Daddy yells.

"Come on, young'uns, and entertain the folks a bit while I finish setting up the wagon."

He makes a big deal of slowly raising the wooden flap on the side and propping it open with a long stick on each end. When folks lay eyes to the rows and rows of elixir for the first time they practically fall all over themselves trying to see. There's more oohing and aahing from the crowd than any one person should have to hear at one time.

Shooting a sneaky sort of look to Filbert, a look that says, "Get to singing, boy," Daddy nods and winks.

And Filbert gets to singing. He instantly breaks into a chorus of "Meet Me in St. Louis, Louis," and Mac and Hazel fill in the harmony, singing louder with each word that spews from their mouths. They dance and sing like nobody's business and once the crowd is at least twenty, twenty-five deep and mesmerized by the show, I look over sort of casual-like and catch Daddy's eye. He gives a subtle nod, not one that anyone but me would notice, and I know that now—for me at least—it really *is* showtime.

"Say there, mister!" I yell, right on cue. "You wouldn't be the man that sells that powerful elixir from the South of France, now would you?"

Daddy's eyes seem as big and round as grapefruits and they're glistening with all the excitement of a baby laying hold to a shiny new rattle. "One in the same, little lady," he shouts. "One in the same."

He grins like he's running for the office of president and needs all the votes he can get.

"And how, pray tell, has a pretty young filly like yourself come to know of my world-famous elixir?"

The crowd separates down the middle just like I reckon the Bible's Red Sea did when Mister Moses waved his staff over the water so's the Israelites could pass through on dry land. And before I know what's happening, Daddy and me are standing there in the middle of that town and that mob staring each other nose hair to nose hair.

"Oh, my granny took some of that elixir a while back," I say loud enough so's everyone there can hear. "She was a-fierce sick, yes she was. Grandpappy said she'd done crossed over into the valley of the never-do-no-good and took to her deathbed for sure. But, one day my grandpappy brung her a bottle of your elixir and now she's out plowing the fields behind our mule. Yes, sir, as sure as I'm standing here living and breathing, Slim's Powerful Franciscan Healing Elixir cured my granny of a fatal case of the can't-help-its."

"Ha! Ha!" Daddy laughs out loud. "I'm not surprised by that a bit, little lady. Not surprised by that at all. Matter of fact, folks," Daddy stretches out his arms to the crowd like he's going to plant a hug on every last one of them, "I hear stories like that everywhere I go."

There's a gleam in Daddy's peacock-blue eyes and a spring to his steps I've not seen since . . . well, since the last crowd he worked. He's jumping around in front of the folks like a caged animal set free.

He's smiling and winking, making goo-goo eyes at the ladies—especially the ones that smell pretty like they just took a bath and slapped on some fancy store-bought perfume.

He's moving in close to the gentlemen, slapping them on the back, shaking their hands, and saying things like "You know what I mean, buddy?" and "I know you've been there—the same as me." Why, when Daddy's out in front of the crowd like he is now, he's so downright charming it almost makes me take a liking to him.

Almost.

I look around and that swarm of folks I'm in the midst of now stands about forty, maybe fifty deep, more than enough for Daddy to draw in a whole mess of money. I move among them, in and out, 'round and around, studying the faces, looking for skeptics and doubters.

That's my job too, you know, to root out the doubters.

Folks that scratch their heads, rub their chins with their hands, or shake their heads with a look of disgust while Daddy's talking. Those are the doubters.

"Now move in close," Daddy says, motioning the crowd closer with a wave of his hand. "Move in close. Folks, this elixir is blended from the purest water that bleeds right out of the hills in the South of France. It's combined with the world's most priceless herbs and minerals." He pulls one of the bottles from the shelf and rubs it between his hands like it's fine gold. "Why, Slim's Powerful Franciscan Healing Elixir is the answer to everything that ails you, from slow digestion to the driest skin."

"Sir?" He points to a man in the crowd. "Are you hard of hearing? And, you," he says, pointing to another, "do you wish your memory was as good as it was when you were the size of one of these darling little children here?" He slings a finger toward Filbert, Mac, and Hazel.

Filbert and Mac bow. Hazel curtsies and grins, showing the empty space where her two front teeth are supposed to be.

Daddy blows her a kiss.

She catches it in midair and pulls it to her chest.

"Ah, aren't they adorable? Well," he shouts, "Slim's Powerful Franciscan Healing Elixir is everything you need to make your life all you've dreamed it could be. Why, one week of this elixir and, men, you'll rise up early feeling fit enough to fill your sheds with enough chopped wood for the winter, plow your fields for the spring, and still race your horse into the barn—all on the same day. Now *that's* some powerful stuff!"

I'm studying their reactions, watching the men poking their thumbs through their button holes and puffing out their chests. Some of the ladies are red-faced and flitting their eyelashes at the men.

"And, ladies," Daddy continues, "you're not left out in the weather. One week of Slim's Powerful Franciscan Healing Elixir and your skin will be smooth as a baby's. Your hair will be full, your eyes will twinkle, and your worry lines will completely fade away."

Daddy hops up the steps of the wagon so's he can be seen by the folks in back, as well as be heard. "Come now, folks, step right on up! Don't be shy! Who'll be the first to try this magnificent miracle-working product? Fifty cents, that's all. Just five silver dimes, fifty copper pennies, or two of our shiny United States quarters—God bless America. A measly pittance to pay for a new life! Come on now, step up. Don't be left out in the cold."

"I'll take a bottle!" an elderly man yells. He waves his quarters in the air.

Hands pop up all over the crowd.

"Sing another song for these fine folks, children, while I serve them up the elixir."

Filbert breaks into a chorus of "The Bear Went Over the Mountain," and the young'uns in the crowd clap and dance along.

Folks are talking amongst themselves, digging in their pockets for change, smiling and nodding while it's all happening. There's money and elixir being passed back and forth faster than a hawk can snatch up a pullet, and if I didn't know better I'd figure my daddy was striking it rich just off this one giant gathering of people.

I scan the crowd again, moving among them, looking at faces and listening to comments. As always, there are a few holdouts, and, just as Daddy's instructed, I make my way through, moving in next to the doubters.

Even in all of the hubbub Daddy keeps his eye on me, and I know—bad as I hate to admit it—he's counting on me to be right with what I see and hear.

I spy a group of three ladies huddled together beneath the skinniest excuse for an oak tree I've ever seen in my life. They're shaking their heads saying something about the entire lot of us going to the devil, with their lips pressed tight and making straight lines across their faces.

Doubters.

I know what to do. I stand my ground and wait.

Daddy notices too, and after a while he moves in for the kill.

12

Daddy Gives the Orders

Daddy snatches three bottles of the elixir from the shelf, shoves one into each pocket, and clutches the third to his chest.

I step aside as he moves in toward the ladies.

He bows in front of them, one arm outstretched to the side like he was bending low before a king or a queen.

The ladies let loose of their lined lips and smile. One giggles.

One at a time, Daddy takes their hands and plants a kiss on top of each. "My, my, my," Daddy begins, and I know in my mind what's coming next. "What beauty I see before me."

I run the words over and over in my mind before they ever seep from his mouth, my lips moving just a tiny bit. After all I've heard this speech so many times I could recite it myself given the chance.

"However," he continues, "in your ravishing beauty I sense doubt. Ladies, am I correct?"

They hem and haw about, obviously searching for the words to respond. As the crowd turns to watch, their faces turn as red as a fresh-pulled radish.

"Now, ladies," Daddy continues. "Lovely, lovely, enchanting ladies. You wouldn't want to be the only ones in this delightful town to miss out on this powerful elixir, now would you?"

They hang their heads and stare at the ground, and I know why. I've seen it before. Daddy's shaming is working.

"There's no telling when we'll be back in your area with this elixir, ladies; perhaps never. You wouldn't want to be the talk of the town, now would you? Why, I can hear your friends and family now. 'You should have bought a bottle of Slim's Powerful Franciscan Healing Elixir,' they'll say. 'I did, and my rumatiz is gone,' others will testify. 'Feel better than I have in years,' I can hear them saying now."

The ladies whisper among themselves, nod, and then hand over the money for the elixir.

"Sing a little bit of that 'Danny Boy,' that I love so much, children," Daddy hollers.

Filbert lets loose on the tune and before too long Mac and Hazel join in, harmonizing just to beat the band. I mean, them young'uns are singing their hearts out better than I've ever heard them sing.

Watching them, I forget my job for a minute, so I'm surprised to hear a voice yell out, "What you're doing here is wrong—stealing from poor folk like you are."

It's a new man who's just joined the crowd.

The sun's going down behind the mountain, the air's got a sudden bite, and folks who was just smiling at Daddy are beginning to tire. All of a sudden, grumbling takes hold and I can feel the tides of kindness turning.

"I think it's awful," a woman in the crowd says to the man standing beside her. "Making those children work for him like he's doing. It's not right, I tell you. It's just not right."

"You've got a point there," the man next to her says. "Hey! You! Elixir man!" he yells. "What you're doing, working those children like you are, it's not right."

Another man, wearing a wide-brimmed cowboy hat, moves to the front of the crowd. With one hand he waves his hat above his head. "Can't you people see what's happening here?" he shouts in a deep southern drawl. He flings an angry finger toward Daddy. "This man is using his own children to rob you people blind. Why, he's no medicine man. He's a thief!"

Before I know it, there's way more angry shouts than happy ones. The yelling from the crowd turns personal—and it's aimed at the triplets.

"Them's the skinniest children I ever did see!"

"Yeah! Clear to see that the elixir man ain't spendin' his money on food for his kin," someone yells.

"Where'd you get them clothes? In a ragbag?"

"It's the 1920s for crying out loud! Buy them children some proper clothes why don't you?"

"This isn't an elixir-selling show! It's a lesson in how to misuse your children!"

In all my days I've never heard such hollering from townsfolk. A lot of times they end up attacking Daddy—in more than half the towns we play, matter of fact—and that makes us feel bad enough, but I've never heard people picking on young'uns this way. Don't they know them babies have feelings? Why in the world don't they just turn and leave? Why do they have to yell and scream hurtful things at 'em?

Filbert stops singing. He's searching the crowd for Daddy with a panicked look on his face.

Hazel, humiliated, buries her head in her hands—and I know as well as I'm breathing what's coming next from her.

Mac looks like he's seen a ghost.

My heart's breaking for them triplets. I want to run the steps, fall over top of the three of them, and keep them safe from the hurt.

But I can't.

I'm not one of them.

Not now.

Not until the crowd's gone home.

Them's Daddy's orders and I've learned the hard way not to disobey my daddy.

Daddy ignores Filbert's looks. And he ignores the crowd's jeers. But it's clear by the look on his face he can tell them folks have turned against him.

He backs up toward the wagon making a move to pack up the show to leave.

"Well, I'm not a man to stay where I'm not wanted," he says, reaching to drop the flap on the side of the wagon to cover the elixir, his face a blotchy cranberry red.

"You know the old saying: You can lead a horse to water, but you can't make him drink of the water he don't want," he says. "You'll be sorry, but I can't make you take a cure you've no need of."

Despite the jeers and Daddy's packing to go, there's folk still reaching out with their money and snatching for the elixir. And Daddy—being the kind of man he is—can't resist.

He shoves his pockets with their quarters, dimes, and pennies, and is handing out bottles of Slim's Powerful Franciscan Healing Elixir in return. All the while the triplets stand huddled in a wad on the steps of the wagon looking like three wilted pansies on a hot summer's day. It seems Daddy don't care if his babies are hurting. Proving what I always say: it's all about the money with him.

I move through the crowd slow but sure, making my way to the front of the wagon without causing a stir or looking conspicuous. Old Stump gives a whinny like she's glad to see me, so I pat her on the side of the head and shush her as best I can.

Moving slowly to the backside of the wagon, I aim to plant myself there until Filbert, Mac, and Hazel come down from the steps and around the backside of the wagon.

Daddy's going to be mad at me for leaving the crowd. But for once I don't care. My heart's aching for the triplets, and right now that's more important than Daddy's old elixir or his money.

The three of them come around back with their hearts shoved clean up into their hands, with Hazel sobbing like she's lost the best doll she ever owned, and the boys looking like they don't know what's hit them.

As I pull them to me, I hear the mumbling of the crowd breaking up. All of a sudden, from out of nowhere, someone yells, "Hey! That girl ain't got no ailin' grandmaw healed by the elixir! She's with the rest of the group. It's a setup. That joker ain't nothin' but a flimflam man! Get him!"

13

HURLING STONES

I'm the first one to see them coming, even before Daddy and the triplets notice. There's six, maybe seven boys, years older than me, toting big sticks and throwing stones at the wagon and at Daddy and at the elixir bottles. The closer they come, the more ruckus they make and the bigger the sticks and stones they throw, breaking some of the bottles into tiny little specks of pieces.

They're shouting at us too; stuff like "Snakes!" "Liars!" "Thieves!" "Crooks!" and "Robbers!" And the louder they shout, the faster and harder them stones they're throwing are hurled.

"Chestnut!" Daddy shouts. He don't have to yell it twice.

"Go! Go! Go!" I shout, shoving the triplets up the steps. "Shut the door, Filbert, quick! And bolt it!"

Seeing that the young'uns are safe, I turn to run to the front of the wagon, intending to go to Old Stump and make

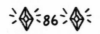

sure she's not too worked up from the ruckus, then climb up and go through the front behind Daddy's seat. But those rocks and sticks are banging against my skin like hailstones on a tin roof. I can't run fast enough to dodge them there's so many, and they're coming so fast. I couldn't have seen where I was going even if I'd had my eyes open. And I didn't.

I run my hand alongside of that wagon like a blind woman searching for a home, feeling every crack and splinter and knothole that's ever had a place in that old rickety red and white circus wagon.

I can hear Old Stump getting more spooked by the minute, whinnying and snorting and dancing about, and Daddy's hollering something, but with the ruckus them sticks and stones and screaming townsfolk are making, there's no way I can make out his words.

I stop a second to look around for Daddy, and all of a sudden, the biggest rock I've ever seen hurled into the air whacks me square on the side of the head before I can duck it. Down I go, landing with a mouth plumb full of dirt and blood.

That's the last I remember until I come to—lying on my cot, staring at the ceiling, and wishing I was anywhere but in the middle of Alabama in the back of a circus wagon with my kin.

Filbert, Macadamia, and Hazel are all standing over me—staring down like they think I'm going to turn flips or do a magic trick right there in the middle of the wagon. I hear voices coming from the outside, and only one of them is a voice I recognize. Daddy's.

"I sure am sorry this happened to your girl, Mister Hill," one of the outside voices says. "We've had trouble from those boys before. They congregate together and do their mischief, then when the law comes they scatter, so we don't have a chance to catch them in the act. I sure hope your daughter is going to be all right."

"I think she will," Daddy says. "The doctor gave her a good going-over. He says she'll have a nasty bruise and a pretty bad headache for a while, but once she heals she'll be as good as new."

"Good," the other man says. "Why don't you folks stick around a few days, just until the girl gets to feeling better? Then you can scoot out of town. We've got laws against peddling things like your elixir, so it's best you be moving on as soon as you can. Me and my boys will keep an eye out while you're here though, just in case those hoodlums come back around. If I were you, I'd keep the little ones close too, if you know what I mean."

"Thank you, sheriff. I will."

The triplets run to the door of the wagon, I reckon to see the sheriff as he's leaving.

"Is Chestnut gonna die?" Hazel asks, still staring out of the door.

"Nope," Mac says. "Daddy says she's too mean to die."

They jump down the steps and I'm glad. My head hurts something fierce, and all I want to do is sleep. But I can't. Or at least I can't sleep long. If we've got to be moving on like the sheriff says, I've got flyers to nail up.

Rolling from my cot, I try to stand, but the hammer in my head kicks the feet right out from under me. I'm back on my cot, and even though I fight it the best I can, I'm drifting off to sleep before I know it.

Later, I'm half-awake but mostly asleep when I feel the bumping of the wagon wheels against the dry, rocky road. Every bump sends a sharp ax up the side of my head like it's going to split open and spill out all my good sense over the floor of this rickety wooden wagon.

As I lie here suffering something fierce from the pain of it all, a powerful thought comes to me. Now, I'm not a baby, and I'm not a sissy by no means, and more than all that, I'm not right proud of what I'm feeling, but well . . . I'll just go ahead and say it.

I want my mama, and I want her now.

Seems when a body is sick or ailing the only thing makes them better is their mama. Their mama's arms to hug them. Their mama's lips to kiss them and rub their aching head with her soft and gentle hand. And more than anything else, an ailing body needs their mama's words to let them know that everything's going to be all right.

But a mama's the one thing I've not got right now.

I wish my daddy would hug and kiss and give me comfort, especially since he's the one who snatched me away from that loving mama.

But he don't.

14

Music and Empty Bellies Don't Mix

The first thing I notice nearly two weeks later when we roll into New Orleans is the smell. Some of the smells are good, some of the smells are stinky, but there's plenty of smells to go around for sure. With my head still pounding from time to time, I breathe deep, filling my lungs to the brim with the aromas of fresh-caught fish, ripe bananas, and hot baked bread. Almost sets a nose to twitching clean off a young girl's face. Matter of fact, if a body hasn't had a meal in a while, their stomach's liable to rub right up next to their backbone, and their mouth will water like a fountain. Won't do no good to ask how I know.

The most curious thing of all though is that folks are eating—right out in the open.

Oh, they're sitting down at tables and chairs of course, but right out on the sidewalks where everyone that passes can see as plain as day what they're eating and wish they had some too. Why, if a girl didn't have control of her arms and hands—like I do, of course—them folks might look up and find half of the food's been snatched clean off their plates.

The way I've got it figured it would just be cutting out the middle man. Instead of having them people waste the food on their plates by not eating all of it, then tossing it over into the trash, I could just reach down and snatch it up before it ever even touches the can.

But I don't.

Wouldn't be proper.

There's too much of Mama in me for that.

There's music in New Orleans too. Everywhere, there's music. Daddy calls it "the jazz."

Seems there's not a street corner or an alleyway where folks aren't blowing on something, beating on something, or plucking and strumming on some strings.

They's dancing right out in the middle of the streets too. Women and men, flipping and flitting and looking like they're twirling around in thin air. It makes a body's mind go to wondering if the whole world's gone plumb crazy, leastwise New Orleans, Louisiana.

I can't recall when I did see so many folks in one place either—all shapes and sizes—but there's only one person I'm looking for, and that's my mama. Every face I see I give a second look, just in case she's come to New Orleans to find us.

Surely she's close. She knows how much Daddy likes warm weather and that he's always talked about going to New Orleans someday. It only makes sense that Mama would have figured out that Daddy would tote us here. But New Orleans is a mighty big place, so how could she ever find us? I never got to nail up my flyers in Birmingham telling her where we'd be, and besides that, she'd not know to look for us in an old circus wagon.

"Come on now, Chestnut," Daddy says. "Keep up with the rest of the family. Don't lollygag behind."

"Keep up with the rest of the family?" What in the world has come over my daddy? I know I was hit on the head, but reckon it's mostly healed by now. Daddy hasn't said those words since he started selling the elixir. Wonder what he's up to? He always makes me stay behind, like he's ashamed of me and don't want me along, like he wishes I wasn't part of the family. He says he can't have folks recognizing me as being with the group on account of the lies he makes me shovel at them. Huh. I think he just don't want to be seen with me. Then again, maybe he's got the conscience all of a sudden— on account of he didn't do any comforting when I got wacked in the head with that rock. Maybe he's—

Filbert interrupts my maybes with a question.

"We gonna do a show here, Daddy?"

"Nope."

Daddy smiles a sneaky sort of grin.

"Nope? How come?" Filbert looks at Daddy and shoves his hands deep into his pockets, just like Daddy.

"Well, son, we're not here to *do* a show. We're here to *make* a show."

Daddy's practically skipping along the street.

"Huh?"

Filbert looks back at me like he thinks Daddy's speaking a foreign tongue.

I shrug. It does set my mind to wondering though. Back on the road from Birmingham, when Daddy asked Filbert if the triplets thought they had done their best in the show, I knew by Daddy's question that he had some tricks up his sleeve. I just didn't have any idea it would be so soon, and way down here in New Orleans, Louisiana, to boot.

As we walk the streets, breathing in smells and listening to the sounds, Daddy's words might have told Filbert we weren't doing a show, but he sure has put on his show face. In a way, he's doing his own show right now just by jumping around and conversing. He's working the crowds like they're there to see him, smiling, waving, and shaking hands with everyone he meets. And he's introducing his young'uns—even me—to folks along the way. Seems to me my daddy's happier than a bald-headed baby with a bonnet.

It's easy to see that the triplets are loving the excitement of New Orleans, too. They're laughing and dancing, whooping and hollering, and twirling around like twisters with a plan.

I never much figured my daddy the kind of man who liked this sort of stuff though.

Fancy three-story high-rising buildings, more people dressed up in store-bought clothes and hats than you can shake a stick at. With anything you could think to name to eat, streetcars running on rails through the middle of the streets, and all of it wrapped up in a tight little package called New Orleans.

We stroll for hours, soaking up the music, saying hey, and being neighborly to folk we've never seen and probably never will lay eyes to again. And, we're breathing in the food of the privileged. My belly's growling worse than a half-starved grizzly staring into a rabbit's den. Feels like I ain't had nothing more than a bite or two of taters or stale biscuits to eat in weeks—not more than just barely enough to keep a cat alive much less a growing girl.

We turn a corner, head down a little side street, and come upon a Negro man picking on the banjo. There's a crowd gathered in front of and around him so we can't see any more than the top of his head—just enough to tell that he's a Negro man with a gift for the music. I mean, I heard some of the finest banjo music you'd ever lay claim to played back in the hills of Kentucky, but this here's different. It's lively enough so's you can shake a leg and dance to, but it's calming and relaxing at the same time; the kind of music that sort of sets a body's mind at ease.

Puts me in the mind of being wrapped up tight in a well-worn patchwork quilt and laid out straight into a great big old bed stuffed plumb full of goose feathers. Now I tell you, life can't get no better than that. Daddy must have thought it too because he slows then stops, like he intends to stay here a while.

We stretch and strain, mesmerized as the man picks his banjo and sings. After a while his music dies back, the crowd parts a ways, and we see the man in the clear for the first time. I can't believe my eyes, and it seems that Daddy is every bit as surprised as me.

It's Mac who speaks first. "Hey, Daddy! That's . . . that's that man that came—"

"Abraham?" Daddy interrupts.

Abraham keeps on plucking his four strings, but he's not singing anymore.

"How are ya'll?" Abraham asks, smiling.

"Mighty fine! Mighty fine," Daddy says. "But how in the world—I mean—"

It seems my daddy's words have left him. A problem he don't often have.

Abraham leans back and laughs out loud. "Bet you neber thoughts you'd see me here, now did you?"

Daddy shakes his head. "How long . . . Why didn't you—"

"How long I been here?" Abraham asks, still strumming away at his banjo. "Moved here after I left de mines. Warmer den Kentucky. Better for de bones."

Daddy nods.

"As for why I didn't tells you where I's headed," Abraham says. "Reckon you neber asked."

"Som'din ya'll likes to hear played?" Abraham asks, smiling real big.

Daddy nods. "Well sure. How about a little of my favorite, 'Danny Boy'? You do know that one don't you?"

"I shore's do, Slim!"

He cuts loose on the banjo strings, plucking and strumming as hard and loud as his fingers will let him go. Then he breaks out singing.

Daddy looks down and catches Filbert's eye, then gives him a nod. Filbert opens up and goes to singing right along with Abraham, just like they've been singing together for years, and just like the whole thing was planned. Not long after, Mac and Hazel join in too.

Part of me wants to step back away from them, like it's showtime and Daddy's going to whip out the elixir bottles at any second. Makes me look around right fast for the doubters too.

But there aren't any.

Matter of fact, folks are gathering all right but it's not from the sounds of an elixir show. It's from a music show.

When they finish their song, Daddy pulls a handkerchief from his pocket and wipes his eyes. I have to look at him twice to see them tears of his are genuine.

Daddy shakes his head, his face the reddish-orangey color of a sunset after a rainstorm. He clears his throat and shoves his hankie deep into his back pocket. "Well, I for one am hornswaggled," he says. "Abraham, I had no idea the talent you possess."

"I like your music, Abraham," Hazel says, smiling and stepping closer to touch his banjo.

"No, Hazel," I say, pulling her away. "You call him Mister Abraham."

"Well, Daddy said we could call him Abraham when we was back in Georgia."

"Maybe *he* did," I say shooting Daddy a look. "But Mama says the most disrespectful thing a young'un can do is call an adult by their first name. You don't want to be disrespectful now, do you?"

Hazel shakes her head.

"How long have you been playing, Abraham?" Daddy drops to one knee, examines the banjo, then looks Abraham in the eyes.

"Aw, more years 'n I care to shake a stick at. I can't b'lieve I never did play in front of you or your kin. Course yo' wife neber did want the likes of me . . ."

His words trail off as Hazel pulls loose from my grip. "So, what do we call you, Abraham?" she asks, shooting me the evil eye back over her shoulder. "Do you have a last name?"

Abraham snickers. "Naw, little one. It's jes' Abraham, like in de Bible. Dat's what all de folks rounds here calls me."

"Mm-hm," Daddy says. He gives Abraham a wink. "Well now, 'just Abraham, like in the Bible,' what do you think about joining us on the road? It don't pay much but it would give you a steady roof over your head and an occasional meal. And being with friends is always better than being on alone. I'd be mighty glad to have another grown person around. Mostly though we could use someone with your talents to brighten up our show."

Abraham leans over and spits into the street. It's then and there that I know without a doubt, he and Daddy are kindred spirits.

"Remind me again, Slim, what kinda show ya'lls have?"

"An elixir show. Slim's Powerful Franciscan Healing Elixir to be exact," Daddy says. "The wagon's parked just outside of town. You'd have to ride up front with me, young'uns got the back. We'll pitch camp and rest along the way. It's a hard life, but a good way to see the country and offer up a bit of help to ailing folk along the way."

Daddy don't notice, but he's set my teeth on edge asking Mister Abraham to come along. He didn't ask us if we minded. And just who does he think he is, offering what little food we've got to someone else?

Daddy shoots Abraham another wink and it starts me to wondering if they've got secrets between them.

Abraham rubs his chin with his hand and stares up into the evening sky, like he's thinking great, important thoughts. His uncut snowy-white whiskers make a scratching sound against the palm of his hand, and for the longest time he don't say a thing.

Without Abraham's picking, the music seems way off in the distance and there's a low humming sound in the air, like the sound of folks talking but not being able to make out the words. Once in a while, there's a shrill cackling that cuts through the air—like the laughter of ladies being happy.

"Well now," Abraham says. "S'pose I might be p'suaded to come along. Where's ya'll be headed next?"

Daddy smiles. "Reckon we'll be working our way into Texas, up through Arkansas, maybe into Missouri." He shrugs. "Just anywhere the wind takes us is where we're headed. No plans really."

Daddy's words are like a big jagged splinter up under my fingernail, throbbing and pounding until it festers up and bleeds. I've had a feeling down deep in my gut that he wasn't aiming to go back to Kentucky. Shucks. My daddy's not even trying to get back to Mama.

While he's standing around jawing with Abraham, and the triplets are dancing in circles and twirling and chasing around and around, I want to let go with them young'uns and have a bit of fun, but I can't. Too much on my mind. Anyway, with Daddy occupied and busy taking care of business like he is, someone's got to be the responsible adult and watch out after them babies.

But while I'm watching, my mind goes to painting this fancy city of New Orleans in all of its fiery flames of orange and fuchsia, red-onion purple, and the deep, dark powdery blues of eggplants. The jazz that Daddy loves so much is a hot

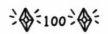

mix of turquoise and aqua and indigo with large splatters of sunshine yellow and splashes of jalapeño green and hydrangea pink.

But the more I think about Daddy offering Mister Abraham a place with us, those sunshine yellows turn to cool icy blues, and the jalapeño greens turn to angry, dark avocado-skin streaks of green. The more Daddy's words swirl around in my brain, the more I wish I had some storm-cloud gray to smear over the top of the brightness, or maybe even some zebra-stripe black just to completely cover up the whole picture in my mind.

Daddy's words have sealed it in my mind. I've just got to get back to Mama. But, them flyers won't work 'til I get to nailing them up, so tonight, when the moon is high and the air full of the sounds of the sleeping, I'll be working on a new plan. Oh, I'll still nail up my flyers, but it's clear to me now that there's got to be more to fixing my family than *just* flyers.

"All right, Abraham," Daddy says, talking loud and jerking my mind back from my plans. "If you decide to join us, be at the wagon in the morning at first light. I'll be happy if you come. I think you'll find it will be beneficial to us both."

We walked a lot more, listened a bit, and smelled our way through the streets of New Orleans, with its oven-pulled hot breads and its crispy skillet-fried chickens, wishing there was just some way under the heavens that we could at least taste some of that food them folks is wasting and fixing to toss over into the trash.

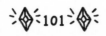

On the way back through town all the triplets would say was, "Daddy when are we leaving?" "Daddy, I'm hungry." "Daddy, can you get us some food?" "Daddy, let's go back to camp and get something to eat."

Poor little things, they can beg all they want but Daddy and me both know the truth. There ain't enough food back at camp to fill up the belly of one person, much less five, and now Daddy's gone and talked to Abraham about coming along with us.

It don't pay much but it would give you a roof over your head and an occasional meal, he said. Huh! Occasional is right.

I'm as mad at my Daddy as a swarm of wasps shut up in a canning jar, and I can hardly wait to get back to camp to open up on him. My anger is raging and I'm not going to be quiet about my feelings this time. The way I see it he'd better hang on to his hat because I've got more than one crow to pick with my daddy before this night is through.

15

Snake!

Filbert, Mac, and Hazel start up the steps to the wagon, but stop the second I light into Daddy.

"I don't understand what you're doing by bringing Abraham on. There's barely enough food for us now, picking up a few things here and there, bumming food from other folks when we can. How are them babies going to get a proper meal when there's another mouth to feed?"

I know he could tell by my tone that I was good and mad, but Daddy don't say a word. Matter of fact, it's as if I wasn't talking to him at all. The triplets are standing with their mouths gaped, like they can't believe I'm talking to Daddy this way.

"Daddy, are you listening to me?" I'm trying not to be disrespectful, but realizing with every word that splurts from my mouth my efforts aren't really working.

He whirls around, cocks his head to one side, and looks me right between the eyes, like maybe I just shot his dog.

Without taking his eyes off me, and soft as a canary with laryngitis he says, "Filbert, Mac, and Hazel, go inside the wagon. This is between me and your sister."

Suddenly I realize by his softness that Daddy must be fixing to unleash his words on me. I swallow hard and take a deep breath, dreading the tongue-lashing that's to come.

"Chestnut Hill, you're getting just a little too big for your britches," he says, slinging a finger toward my face. "It seems to me like it hasn't been long since we had this talk and now here we are again, going down this same rocky path."

"Daddy—"

"Just hush." He touches his finger to his lips and shakes his head, but Daddy's not seen what I have.

"But, Daddy—" I gasp and then slap my hands over my mouth.

"I said, hush."

Moving only my eyes I give an exaggerated stare toward the ground hoping Daddy will follow where I'm looking.

Finally, he sees it and freezes. Crawling across his shoe is the biggest copperhead I've ever seen in all my twelve years of living.

"Don't. Move."

He needn't worry. I've got way too much fear inside.

I remind myself to breathe and then quietly let out the breath as the snake crawls off his shoe and underneath the bushes, in a moseying, meandering sort of way. We both let out a long sigh.

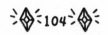

"That was close," he says.

"Yes, sir. It was."

"Chestnut, come over here and sit down with me."

He motions to the large log beside the fire. Fearing his words nearly as much as another snake, I sit and stare into the fire.

He waits a long while before he speaks; matter of fact I'm beginning to believe all he wants is my company. I couldn't be more wrong.

"Let me ask you a question," he says. "And I want you to think before you speak. Have any of you young'uns ever starved to death? Oh now, I don't mean gone to bed hungry—I know you've done that—but I mean gone without food so long you've gotten sick or one of you has died?"

"No, sir."

He clears his throat and stares into the fire. "Have you ever seen me sit down to eat and not share with you or the triplets?"

"No, sir."

"Have you ever known me not to take care of your needs? Now not your wants," he turns to face me, "but your needs. You do know the difference, don't you?"

I swallow hard. "Yes, sir, and no, sir, I haven't."

"You haven't what? Mac, get back in the wagon right now!" he hollers, never turning to look back over his shoulder.

How does he do that? How does he know what's going on behind him without looking?

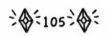

I shake my head. "No, sir," I say. "I've never known you not to get us what we need."

"Yes, so what in the world makes you think I'd start now? Why, all of the sudden, do you think I'd allow a stranger to come in here and take food out of the mouths of my babies?"

I shrug, but still, in my heart, I'm not convinced.

Then Daddy does something a might curious—something he hasn't done in years since Mama left—or I should say, since he stole us away.

He puts his arm around me and pulls me close.

I don't know whether to jerk away or cry, but I reckon now's not the time for either, so I sit still as a tree, and let him hug me. But I don't hug him back. I can't. No way I can let myself care about him.

Then, with his arm still wrapped around my shoulder, he takes a finger and pushes my chin up so's we're staring nose hair to nose hair. He talks so softly, and for the first time in a long time I get a funny feeling inside—a funny feeling that maybe I've been wrong about him caring for us after all.

"Chestnut, you four are my children, and I'll do whatever I have to do to take care of my children. There might not always be as much food around as I'd like for there to be, and it might not always be what you would want to eat, but you haven't starved to death yet and I'm not aiming to let you starve to death in the future. Now, you and I both know we're not like these city folk—caring only for ourselves and never

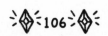

being concerned with the needs of others. We Hills are always open to sharing what we've got with others, aren't we?"

I nod, suddenly feeling as small as a fairyfly.

"You know the same as me that the only thing that matters in this old world is what we can give away to others. And Abraham is an 'others,' isn't he?"

"Yes, sir."

I know he's right—about the caring for others that is—but in my heart I don't think his words are matching up with what I know to be true about him. He's all about the money. He's not concerned about taking in Abraham—even if he is an old friend from back home—sharing our food, and giving away to others. All he cares about is what that banjo-picking man can do for him, to put more money in his pockets.

My words say, "Yes, sir," but not my heart, where it counts.

"Now, get on up in that wagon and climb into bed."

He smiles, and before I can stop myself, I smile back.

"Yes, sir."

Now, I'll be the first to admit that when he wants, Daddy can be a charming man, full of eye twinkle, fancy words, and tender feelings. But that don't sway me. Mama says the proof of how much someone cares is in the way they treat you. Stealing young'uns away from their home, leaving their mama pining away and worrying says more to me than Daddy's words ever could.

So, when the air is full of the sounds of the sleeping, by the light of the kerosene lamp I draw up more flyers with the next

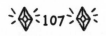

town listed in Daddy's black book: Beaumont, Texas. When I'm done, I snatch up Daddy's hammer, fill my pockets with his nails, and shimmy off away from the wagon and back into town.

Strangest thing I ever did see too. Seems like the only ones asleep in the big, old city of New Orleans is my kinfolk. I walk—and run—by more eating, drinking, entertaining places than I ever seen in my life, wishing in my mind I could stop a while and paint the likes of it all, but I've got no time for that. I run fast as I can from street light to street light, nailing flyers to every pole in town and on the way, to keep my mind off my fears, I think about getting back to Mama.

Seems to me that there's only one way I'm going to get that happy-ever-after home I want, and that's by grabbing the bull by its horns. The way I see it, if Mama can't come to me, I might just have to leave Daddy and run away to get back to her.

16

STRANGERS MOVING IN AND STAYING

Morning brings a new but familiar voice around the campfire.

Filbert, Mac, and Hazel jump off their cots and spring out the door with all the energy of a herd of three-legged kangaroos. Me? Well, it was all I could do to get my eyes to open after the long and tiring night I had, running and sneaking through downtown New Orleans like a rabid fox on the hunt for its next bite.

"Morning, Mister Abraham," I hear the triplets say in unison.

"How are ya'll?" is his reply.

Stumbling out the door, I join them around a big fire in the middle of camp.

"Chestnut, Abraham's come to join us. Aren't you going to speak to him?"

"I'm sorry, morning, Mister Abraham," I say, still wiping night grit from the corners of my eyes.

He and Daddy are sipping coffee and laughing like all the miles between them never happened. I'm not glad he's come, but now that he's here, reckon I might as well make the best of it.

There's nothing much to do in the early morning light but sit and stare across the campfire. It's here, hugging to the warmth of the popping fire that I get my first real, up close look at Abraham.

He's scruffy, with rough-looking whiskers across his chin and halfway up his face, which I had noticed before. And he's got the whitest, straightest teeth I ever did see in my life. He's stooped and bent at the shoulders, and I suppose now that I see him clearly and can think through it all, it must be from many years leaning over the banjo and plucking. His hands are knobby and twisted and tremble a bit when he reaches, but his voice is soft and welcoming. And he smiles—the sort of smile that makes you want to trust him with every secret you've ever had.

"Mawnin', child," he says, nodding.

"So is it true, Mister Abraham?" asks Hazel. "Are you really going on the road with us?"

"Dat's all right wit ya'll, ain't it?"

"Yay!" Hazel hollers.

"You bring your banjo?" Filbert asks.

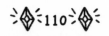

"Sho' nuff did, child. Right over dere," he says, pointing to the banjo propped against the trunk of a tree with one crumpled brown paper sack beside it.

"Can we sing with you? Can we sing something now?" Mac asks.

"All right, young'uns," Daddy says. "Don't bombard Abraham with your begging. There'll be plenty of time for singing once we get on the road. Come on, boys, help Abraham get his things loaded into the wagon. We'll break up camp and be on our way."

For the next three weeks, we bump along, Abraham sitting by Daddy, strumming and picking on his banjo as we ride. And there's singing, lots and lots and lots of singing, with Abraham taking lead and the triplets harmonizing right along. I pat my foot in time with the music and hum along just as soft as a cockroach scatting from sunshine. I can sing as good as the rest of them—maybe better—but there's no way I want Daddy thinking I'm happy enough to have the music in me.

I spend my time working on my new plan and drawing—landscapes mostly—but not of Louisiana land, or even Texas, but of Kentucky, with its cornstalk-green hills and rolling meadows that stretch out for miles, dotted like a face of freckles with wild strawberries, furry dandelions, and dragonflies, just the way I remember it all.

When Daddy finally pulls the wagon into Beaumont, Texas, we're all more than ready for a rest from the road.

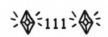

Abraham and Daddy—frightfully happy to have another man along—hop from the wooden seat up front and begin to set up camp. Mama says jawing at young'uns all day is the fastest way to make a grown person's brain turn to mush. Reckon Mister Abraham being here will help Daddy get rid of his mush.

"We gonna do a show here, Daddy?" Mac asks, not bothering to stop running and chasing Hazel and Filbert 'round and around the wagon.

"Yes. Yes, I believe we will."

Daddy props his hands on his hips and bobs up and down on his toes. He looks around slowly, then stretches and yawns. "No time like the present to try out the new act, isn't that what you say, Abraham?"

"Sho' nuff do, Slim. Sho' nuff do."

Daddy's come to life again. He's smiling and patting Abraham on the back and there's a spring to his step that only comes when he's doing a show. He jumps around the wagon, stacking wood, brushing Old Stump, and even joining in a game of chase with the triplets.

He unbolts the door to the side of the wagon where he stores the elixir and runs his hands across the bottles, turning each one of them so's the labels all line up and face the front. Then he lets the lid down on the bottles extra careful like and throws the bolt across. He smacks himself on the chest, like he's telling all the world he's mighty proud of what he's done, and lets out a long sigh.

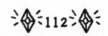

"All right, Abraham, let's go into town for a bit, sort of check out the prospects while we gather supplies. We'll just leave the fire until we return, hmm? Chestnut, you and the babies come too, but you remember to hang back away from the rest of us."

Daddy's talking fast.

And loud.

Too loud for my morning headache, and I notice right off it don't take Daddy long to get back into the same old routine of acting like I'm not one of the family. But no matter. I've got my brand-new plan in mind.

Maybe, just maybe, I'll become a jumper and jump onto a passing train heading back to Kentucky. Or maybe I can find someone in the next town who'll let a strong girl like me work for them for a while—just until I can save up some money for a bus ticket. If the flyers don't work, I mean.

I tag along same as usual, and when we get to the general store, I scatter.

The triplets handle everything they see, as usual, causing me to come close to dying of fright right there in front of them all.

Abraham and Daddy are loading up supplies.

"Excuse me, sir," Daddy says to the man behind the counter. "Where do you keep your nails? Seems I've misplaced mine. Used to have a box plumb full but I couldn't find a one of them this morning. I suppose I've let them spill out somewhere along the way."

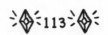

Daddy's babbling on and on with his words, trying to make best friends of everyone he meets.

The man behind the counter takes money from the customer beside Daddy and then slides the bills into the cash drawer. He leaves the cash register door wide open and moves from behind the counter, showing Daddy to the nails.

As they walk to the back of the store I take a quick look around.

There's not a soul in sight. Daddy, Abraham, and the man are clear to the back of the store. Triplets are leapfrogging and chasing each other, not paying a flea's bit of attention to me, and there's not another customer anywhere in sight.

If there ever was a chance, it's now.

I move quick, but quiet, inching my way behind the counter and keeping my eye on the man with Daddy and Abraham the whole time.

He never turns to look. None of them do, and Daddy's keeping him occupied, just like if we'd had the whole thing planned.

I scoot close beside the cash register and snatch a fast look at the money. Paper money! They's more of it in that drawer than I've ever seen in one place in my life. I reach for it quick as a flash, but lose my nerve and jerk my hand away empty.

All of a sudden and quick as a flash my head's so full of thinking that it hurts.

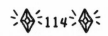

Stealing is wrong and you know it. Don't do it. The Bible says it's one of the big ten don't-do commandments that the preacher talks about. You'll go down to the devil for sure if you steal.

Funny thing is though, quick as them thoughts come to me, a whole other set slides in right behind, pushing them out of the way.

But you need that money to buy a train ticket to get back to your mama. Girl being with her mama's not wrong. Girl going back to where she was when she got snatched away from her home's not wrong. Stealing's wrong but only if you don't have a good enough reason.

Chestnut Hill, get to moving!

You've got a good enough reason!

17

MURDERING KIN

Right then and there, behind that counter in the front of that general store, the devil takes me over completely, mind and body.

I reach up and grab the biggest old handful of money my bony hands will hold, and then I shove that money all the way down into the bottom of my pocket. Moving fast, I skedaddle from behind the counter and slip away, trying as best as I can to act like I've not done one thing wrong.

My heart's beating into my throat, my mouth is parched, and my hands are sweating like the outside of a glass of ice in the summer sun. And I think for sure my knees are aiming to quiver and vibrate and wobble clean out from underneath me at any second.

All I want to do is run!

Run from the store and never show my face in this town again—or anywhere else for that matter.

I don't catch Daddy's eye to let him know I'm going to run. I don't tell the triplets I'm leaving, and I don't tell Abraham. I just head straight for the door, grasping tight to my pocket and the paper money that's shoved down inside.

He didn't lay eyes to me, but I know the man in the back of the store with Abraham and Daddy knows what I've done. My mind's already got him hot on my heels, chasing me out of the store.

Suddenly I trip and about fall flat on my face.

Long as I live and breathe I'll never forget seeing them cans with red and white labels and fancy black letters falling to the floor—one by one—and landing into a heap on the wide pine boards beside the table. Who knew cans could fall so slowly and yet so fast at the same time?

If I could find a way to believe that God wasn't going to open up the heavens, snatch me up by the neck, and sling me straight to the devil for stealing, I could pray for the floor to swallow me where I am.

But I can't.

I can't pray because I know in my heart that I broke one of them Ten Commandments the preacher back home in Kentucky hollers about. Now I'm not only in trouble with the man behind the counter in back of the store, and with the sheriff, and with my daddy soon as he finds out what I done, but I'm in trouble with God, and that's the worst trouble of all to be in.

Beneath the table I crawl, slipping and sliding over the cans, not quite sure whether to pick them up, or just

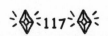

go to running. Picking up the cans I knocked down is the respectable thing to do, but if I do, the man with Daddy and Abraham will have the time to see the money's gone. If I don't pick up what I knocked over though, someone might fall and get hurt. Oh, why does my mind always have to be troubled with these conflicting conflicts?

The breath's being sucked out of my body little by little and I can't breathe any better than a dying woman with the death rattles, but I finally come to one conclusion. There's nothing left to do but run.

So I do—out the front doors of the store, down the street, and out of town toward the wagon.

When I get close enough to lay eyes to the wagon, my mind goes to my metal box under my cot. Nobody knows where it is but me, and it's a sturdy one too—found it up near the mines when I was a kid and kept it with me ever since. I keep my treasures in it, a couple of buttons, my found change, and well . . . now . . .

I dart up the stairs, bolting the door behind me. The box slides easily from under my cot. I jerk the money from my pocket and cram it into the box, slam the lid, and shove the box all the way back, next to the wall. Then I sit, fold my hands across my lap, and wait.

I wait for the sheriff.

I wait for lightning to strike me dead and to come face to face with the devil.

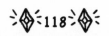

But mostly I wait for my daddy, knowing any second now he's going to bang his fist against the door of this wagon and holler at me to come outside.

Until they come though, there's nothing to do but think. And wait—and let me tell you now, waiting is worse than running.

I can't believe what I've done.

Oh, it was wrong, there's no doubt about that, but then again, I just have to get back to my mama. I know if I can get to her she'll give Daddy the dickens for snatching us up the way he did.

She'll straighten out Daddy's mind and take all of us back to Kentucky. We'll live there the rest of our days, loving each other, and being a real family.

No. I had no choice about what I done, but still I wonder: If I done something against what the preacher preaches but it was for the right reasons, is it still wrong?

They're coming.

Reckon the sheriff's with them.

I go to swallowing, trying my best to gulp down my fears. Trouble is, it don't seem to be working. In fact it's mighty hard to swallow down and suck in air at the same time.

Listening close, I hear the babies rushing for the camp. It sounds like they're laughing. Poor babies, they'll change their tunes when they find out what I've done. They'll be a-fierce disappointed in me for sure. Daddy and Mister Abraham are

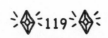

close too. There's the heavy clomping of Daddy's boots and Mister Abraham's talking loud.

The closer they get, the faster my heart beats. My mouth is so dry that if I didn't know better I'd think I'd been sucking on a piece of stale bread with nothing to wash it down. Oh, if only I could suck in a deep breath I know I'd feel better but the air don't seem to be going any farther down than the back of my throat.

I jump up and unbolt the door so's they can get in.

Mama says if you do something you ought not do, best to own up to it and take your punishment.

I hope the sheriff don't come in shooting. Reckon going to jail is a might better than getting shot and meeting my Maker with thoughts of stealing fresh on my mind.

"Chestnut?" Daddy hollers. "Chestnut, you here?"

I sling wide the door expecting the sheriff and the man behind the counter, but they're not here. And what's more, Daddy don't act like he knows a thing.

Then it hits me.

He's acting like he don't know what I done so's I'll come crying to him, begging and pleading for him to fix it and make it all better, same as a baby would do.

Well it won't work.

I won't come crying to him.

I made my bed—just like he says about my mama— and I can lie in it same as anyone else who done something wrong.

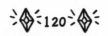

I peek through the doors and look around, expecting a lynching mob to string me up by my heels. They're not here either.

"Why did you run out so fast?" Daddy asks.

"Yeah, you missed a good show!" says Filbert. "A whole table full of soup fell to the floor. Looked to me like the store owner was going to cry. If it wasn't so funny, I'd almost feel sorry for him."

"Me too," says Mac. "Until Daddy made us help him pick up every last one of them cans. Then I felt sorry for us."

They laugh—Daddy, Abraham, and Hazel too.

But I'm not laughing.

Matter of fact, I can barely stand my knees are knocking so.

"Probably good you left when you did, Chestnut. We're doing a show this afternoon and best no one sees you with us," Daddy says. "Oh, by the way, I need a haircut. Need to look my best for the folks, you know. Pull the scissors from my tool box under the front seat of the wagon and come on over here and give my hair a trim."

"I can't."

I say the words without hesitating.

"What do you mean, you can't? Go on now, get them scissors and be quick about it." With a wave of his hand he motions me toward the box.

"Daddy, please. Not right now."

"What do you mean? You've done this hundreds of times. Come on now, there's no time like the present."

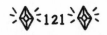

"But, Daddy—"

"Chestnut Hill," he interrupts with his hands planted squarely on his hips, "you're wasting time and time is something we're in short supply of. Quit your hesitating. What's the matter with you? You're acting plumb sheepish."

I don't answer and I don't dare look him in the eyes.

No way I can tell Daddy the truth. No way I can tell him my hands are shaking worse than a hairless cat in a windstorm. I'm just sick, and I reckon what's ailing me won't get well anytime soon.

Spending more time looking over my shoulder for the sheriff than watching where I'm headed, I trip over a stump and stumble all the way to the front of the wagon. I look back, expecting to be laughed at, but no one's paying any mind.

Daddy's perching himself on a tall stump next to the wagon and shaving his cheek with a straight razor. An old tin can lid he's buffed to a shine with shoe polish is propped on a rock in front of him—tilted just so to make a mirror.

He's stubborn as an ox and he'll sit there all afternoon if he has to, waiting for me to get to his haircut. He needs a haircut all right. It's long and shaggy and well over his ears and collar, and there's one long wisp of gray falling limp over his left eye that he blows away with a puff of air from a twist of his mouth.

I pull out the tool box and quickly rummage through it. There's everything in here from a hammer to gauze bandages, from bolts and screws to an extra fork. There's even a needle and spool of thread and a few tiny nails, but what I don't see is scissors.

"What's taking you so long?"

"They're not here."

"What?"

"The scissors are not here!"

He jumps from the stump and walks to the front of the wagon, and he don't take his time. With his hand he swishes around in the tool box, grabbing hold to the scissors, jerking them out of the box, and waving them through the air over his head.

"What's this, Chestnut?" he yells, half his face still covered in mug shaving cream.

"Scissors?"

"Scissors!" Daddy shakes his head like a dog slinging off creek water. "I don't know what's wrong with you, girl. Your mind is somewhere else besides here with the lot of us. Now come on over here and get to cutting. I've not got all day."

"Yes, sir."

I walk up behind him and let out a long breath he can't help but hear.

"Something wrong?"

"No, sir."

"Well then, quit your huffing and get to cutting."

"Yes, sir."

I raise the scissors to his neck and clip, snipping more at the air than his hair.

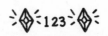

The first few snips are fine, even though my hands are trembling worse than Abraham's, but along about the fourth or fifth snip, reckon I just got a little too close to Daddy's head.

Daddy roars.

"Chestnut! You cut me! You've cut my ear clean off my head!"

He slaps his hands to the side of his head and staggers over to the water bucket—blood spewing from between his fingers. Not a little bit of blood either—it's a gusher!

"Get my ear! Somebody pick up my ear off the ground!" he hollers, waving a finger around in the air to whoever's looking his way.

I throw the scissors into the grass and then I snatch handful after handful of elixir bottles from the side of the wagon, slinging them onto the ground, busting them to smithereens. I holler as loud as I can as I'm slinging and busting, "I told you I couldn't do this right now!"

I have to run.

I'm not rightly sure where I'm running to. I can't go back to town; the whole lot of them's probably looking for me by now.

But I can't stick around here. From the looks of that blood, I've killed my daddy.

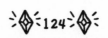

18

Do They Hang Murderers
or Shoot Them?

Daddy's dead, and I killed him.

He made me a liar and I made myself a thief. Reckon it's only natural that murder be the next step. Mama says if you give a body enough rope, it'll hang itself. Reckon that's what I've done for sure—hung myself by my own actions.

My mind can't shake off all the blood I saw spurting out and running down Daddy's arm into his shirt sleeve. Never in my whole life have I seen that much blood. Well, maybe once, when Grandpa Hill killed that goat, but that's a whole other story, and since just the thought of it makes my insides quiver, I'm not likely to tell it anytime soon.

Seeing Daddy bleeding puts the fear in me. Just think, I'm the one that's done him in for good.

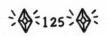

I run along the creek bank, far away from where Daddy's set up camp.

Filbert follows. "Chestnut! Chestnut, wait!"

"Go back, Filbert!"

"But, Chestnut, I—"

"*Go! Back!*"

He chases me for a bit, until I snatch a look over my shoulder and see him standing still with his chin hung down to his chest. It's then that I reckon he's given up and is turning back. I keep running though, until my legs feel like watery jelly.

What are them babies going to say when they see the sheriff hauling their big sister off to jail?

Do they hang murderers or shoot them?

Thing for me to do now is get out of town—and fast—but how can I when he's counting on me to get the triplets dressed proper and point out the doubters for the show? Then again, if Daddy's dead, I reckon it don't much matter, now, does it?

If only Mama were here, she'd know what to do.

But if Mama were here, I wouldn't be in this fix.

Still though, she'll be a-fierce disappointed in me when they do track her down. When she hears I'm in jail she'll cry her eyes out, especially when she finds out they're gonna hang me for thieving and murdering.

Just thinking about my mama brings pools of water to my eyes, but I swallow them back. No way I can sit here on the creek bank feeling sorry for myself, not when there's a heap of planning to do.

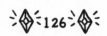

Oh, how I wish I hadn't done it. None of it.

Here I am, not but twelve, and I've already committed two of the don't dos on the list of the big ten.

"Thou"—that means me—"shall not"—that means don't you dare do it—"steal."

Oh my, and then there's the murdering part. Don't kill! The Good Book can't be more plain about that. What I done can't be more wrong.

When I saw that money drawer open and all that paper money poking out, why didn't I just turn and run? Why didn't I listen to the voice in my heart that reminded me stealing was wrong, instead of the one in my head that wanted the train ticket back to Mama?

Reckon I'll be joining my daddy—since I killed him, you know—in the place where they hand out payment for the wrongs we've done in this life. He's probably facing down the devil right now, getting his just reward.

Tired of running, I plop down on the creek bank and stare into the water. They's a stiff wind whooshing through the trees and shuffling the puffy clouds around in the robin's egg–colored sky. Sort of day makes a girl want to kick off her shoes and crawl her toes over mossy green rocks in icy waters up to her knees. The kind of day just right for threading a slimy, fresh-dug earthworm over a rusty hook, slinging it over into the water, and coaxing a speckled brook trout onto the line, and later, tossing it into a black, wrought iron skillet just for frying up crispy, and eating—if a girl had nothing but time on her hands and a clear conscience, that is.

From out of nowhere it seems, Filbert stomps up behind me, huffing and puffing, sucking in air, and coming close to scaring the evil clean out of me.

"Chestnut?"

"Filbert, you scared the life out of me. I told you to go back."

"You . . . ain't . . . my . . ." He's leaned over with his hands propped on his knees.

"Stop. Just stop. Sit down and catch your breath." I reach out, take his hand, and jerk him down beside me.

He props back on his elbows and it seems like forever before he catches his breath. When he finally does commence talking again, I'm wishing he was still panting and unable to talk.

"Chestnut, you hurt Daddy."

"What? What did you say?"

"You hurt Daddy."

Hurt! He said hurt, not killed! I let my body go limp trying not to let on to Filbert that I thought I'd done Daddy in.

"Why?"

"Huh?" I ask, fishing around for more time so's I can answer his question right proper.

"Why did you hurt him?"

I stare across the water into the bushes on the other side.

"I didn't mean to hurt him."

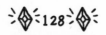

"All he wanted was a haircut, and you cut his hair all the time."

I shrug. "I know, it's just that my hands was shaking so. I told him I couldn't cut his hair right then but he made me. I wouldn't hurt him on purpose, Filbert."

"You sure?" His words ain't matching up with his look. His words say he thinks I'm lying, but his look says, "Can I have a puppy, please?"

"What do you mean? Of course I'm sure. What kind of a question is that?" My face is as hot as a fresh-pulled log from a fire.

He kicks off his shoes. "Well, I just wondered." He runs toward the creek. "'Cause it seems to me like you been mad at him for a long time."

"Roll up your pants before you get in that water!" I yell.

If looks could kill, now he'd be the murderer.

"So, are you mad at Daddy?" he asks, splashing in water up to his waist, tossing it by the handfuls over his head.

The trouble with Filbert is he's too smart to forget things, and I can't take his mind off conversations like with Hazel and Mac.

"I'm not mad." I say it, but I don't believe my own words.

Filbert pulls up rocks from the creek bottom and flips them across the top of the water, trying his best to make them skip, like Daddy can. After a while he spurts out another question. One I don't rightly know how to answer, leastwise not without thinking about it something fierce first.

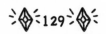

"Do you like Daddy?"

I swallow down the lumpy mess in my throat. How do I answer a question like that? How can I tell a seven-year-old all I'm feeling about his daddy, the same daddy he looks up to and respects? Even if I could get the words out of my mouth, no way he would understand.

"What? Of course I—"

"'Cause I don't think you do." He spits out a mouthful of creek water. "I mean, you don't ever smile at him and you don't even say nice things to him."

For the first time, I realize my little brother's got wisdom in his head that's way past his years. Matter of fact, he's putting the fear in me because I'm thinking maybe, just maybe, he's a whole lot smarter than me.

"Filbert, you don't . . . I mean . . . well . . . oh, forget it. You wouldn't understand. You're too young. We shouldn't be talking about this anyway. It's adult stuff."

"Maybe, but you ain't an adult. You're a kid, same as me."

"Am not."

"Are too."

"Am not!"

"All right, you two, that's enough."

It's Daddy. He's come up behind us, and for once I'm happy he's here. Least I know for sure I'm not a murderer.

I reckon he's here to bring us back to the wagon, but I'm not going. Leastwise, not yet. I hang my head and look away, wondering how much of our conversation Daddy's heard.

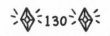

"Filbert, get your shoes on and get back to the wagon. I need to talk to Chestnut."

"But, Daddy—"

"Now, Filbert."

"Yes, sir."

He grabs up his shoes and heads back toward the wagon, but not before he slings the loose water from his hands and arms—and pants—onto me.

I'd whack him on the bottom, but he's already broke into a run.

Daddy sits down next to me but don't say a word, and I realize he's waiting 'til Filbert is clean out of sight. Goodness, I hope he's not going to make me suffer through another one of his long silence sessions.

19

Floppy Hats

Chestnut, you want to tell me what's going on with you?"

I stare at the yellowy greens of the grass and the browns and tans and grays of the rocks along the creek. I watch the tiny red ants, running to and fro, hard at their work, and wonder what their home looks like underground. Matter of fact, I wish I was an ant right now so I wouldn't have to deal with Daddy's question.

"Chestnut?"

I don't answer. Maybe, just maybe, if I ignore him, he'll stop asking.

But I know better.

"Perhaps you'd like to tell me why you decided to have an elixir-busting party. That little display of temper cost me money, young'un. Is that what you want? Are you trying to make me pay for something, some wrong I've done that you're not bothering to tell me about?"

I don't dare look up. Instead I stare at his brown, ankle-high work boots, comfortably broke in and a tad muddier than usual. He worked three days hauling rocks for a neighbor for them boots.

How can I tell him the truth: that all I want is to go home and that I don't believe his stories about Mama? I should be playing with my own friends, drawing landscapes, and learning how to be a real woman, not playing nursemaid to three little babies.

How can I say, "Daddy, I'm sick and tired of trying to wash your lies off in muddy creeks." My belly's growling and sometimes it's hard to think from the hunger, but I shouldn't have to out and out tell him that. He ought to know it by now.

What words can I use to tell him how I hate wearing clothes that aren't my own, laying my head down in towns I don't even know the name of, and then getting up and running to another before the sun sets on the next day?"

What's the best way to tell him I been putting up flyers in every town so's Mama can track us down and find us when she comes looking? And what's more, that I pray—every night—that she really is looking for us.

Do I just come right out and say, "Daddy, I stole money from that store to buy me a train ticket to Kentucky, to get back to my mama, and fix our family up proper?"

No.

I can't.

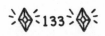

I can't say none of that, so I don't say nothing at all. I just grit my teeth and stare out over the water.

"Are you sick?" he asks.

Still I don't say anything. I cock my head and look into his eyes, so dark they're almost black, and it seems like they almost twinkle in the sunlight. Daddy's not a big man, but what there is of him is as strapping and strong as any man I've ever laid eyes to. I turn away and sit there biting my lip until I feel it starting to swell, hoping he won't ask any more questions, especially one's I'm not about to answer.

I try my best to turn his words off in my mind, to just stop hearing him talk, but it don't work and before too long he starts in again.

"Is it a . . . how should I say it, a . . . a . . . well, is it a woman thing? I mean, do you need another woman to talk to, 'cause if that's it, I can find one in the next—"

I interrupt by shaking my head.

Out the corner of my eye I see him hang his head. Reckon actually talking to me for a change must be a hard thing. Makes me almost feel a might sorry for him.

Almost.

"Are you sure you're not sick or needing—"

I swallow back tears. My insides are shaking so that all I want to do is run.

Somewhere. Anywhere. But no way I can tell him that either, so I don't say anything.

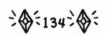

We sit, for the longest, watching speckled trout surface, swallow up mosquitoes or gnats, then shimmy and shake through the shallows for the deeper waters of the creek.

I was about the triplets' age the last time Daddy spent any time alone with me. Matter of fact it was on a creek bank just like this one, and we was fishing. Just the two of us. No triplets. No Abraham. Not even Mama. Just Daddy and me.

Mama always saw to it that I had papers and pencils close, and while I waited for them fish to bite, I drew. After a while of looking over my shoulder watching my pencil make scratches against the paper, Daddy asked what I was drawing. Reckon my pictures weren't as clear back then as they are now.

I told him it was a picture of me, sticking my feet into the ocean water in front of my house by the sea, drawing and painting and living happily ever after like in fairy tales.

Daddy leaned a-way back and laughed, and then he asked just where in the world I thought I'd get a house by the ocean way up here in the hills and hollers of Kentucky. But it was a nice kind of laugh.

We sat there for hours, waiting for our lines to pull and watching dragonflies flit across the water. Daddy chewed on a piece of hay and told me stories most of the day. Mama had packed us a picnic lunch. Nothing special, just a peanut butter sandwich on two slices of fresh baked bread, and an apple. But that was back when he loved me. Back when he didn't

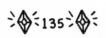

wish I belonged to someone else. Back before he snatched me away from my loving mama and our happy home.

"We best get back," he says now, interrupting my thoughts after a while. Reckon he finally got tired of asking questions and getting no answers. "Time to get ready for the show."

He stands and waits, and after a bit I realize he's waiting for me. He stretches out his hand and I think, *Do I want to take it or not?* And I do, because I'm not aiming to hurt anybody's feelings, not even Daddy's.

"Look," he says, pointing to the side of his head and grinning. "Still got my ear. You didn't take the whole thing off, just shortened it a bit."

He's wrapped his entire ear in what looks to be a piece of cloth—maybe one of his old T-shirts. There's a string circling his ear and it's tied in a knot at the top. Any other time I'd bust out laughing, but not now. Reckon they's too many conflicting feelings inside for that.

He snickers and lifts my chin with his finger so's we're looking at each other eyeball to eyeball but I don't snicker. I just can't. After all, I've still got the picture in my mind of the sheriff coming 'round to haul me off to jail for stealing. What will Daddy do then? What'll happen to the triplets? What will Mama say when she hears?

"You do still remember how to work the crowd, don't you?"

I nod.

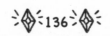

"Good, 'cause you know I'm counting on you. I mean, I can't do the show without you. Someone's got to spot the doubters."

"Yes, sir."

He puts his hand on my shoulder but I pull away. No way I want him thinking one little asking-how-I-am is going to make up for years of not caring. Anyway, I don't believe he cares about me down deep, where it counts—least, not like he did before the triplets come along.

We walk the rest of the way without a word, but all the while my mind's running in circles like a dog chasing its tail.

"Family's back together, Abraham," Daddy says as we saunter into camp. Then all of a sudden, like turning on a fancy, store-bought 'lectrical switch or striking a match to light a candle, Daddy's jumping around like a chicken with its head cut off, ready for the show to begin.

I look at Abraham, going about his business, acting like he never even noticed I'd been gone.

"Let's get this show started," Daddy shouts, practically jumping up and down, his face glowing like a full moon at midnight.

"Dat's fine, and it's sho' nuff good to see's de two o' you. I's ready for de show, Slim."

Hazel runs to me, with a mile-wide smile on her face, and grips my hand. She pulls me along and leads me up the steps and into the wagon, looking up into my eyes the whole time.

"Chestnut, come and see. I can draw just like you."

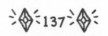

"What do you mean, draw *just like me*? Did you get into my papers? Did you get my stuff?"

Her smile is gone and in its place there's an uncommon fear in her eyes. Hazel never has been one to get a lot of rebuke, so when it does come it puts a fear in her that pops out all over her face.

I look to her cot. Papers, lots of papers—some with pictures of the wagon and Old Stump on them, and some of the papers I hadn't yet turned into flyers—strewn all over the floor and around. Pictures and words I drew ready to tell Mama where we been. Pictures and words to tell her where we're going next.

I ball up my fists and grit my teeth so tight I can almost feel them crumbling like sand inside my mouth.

"Hazel Ophelia Hill. What. Did. You. Do."

It's not enough that my whole body's shaking and trembling worse than a duck feather caught up in a twister, but now the anger's boiling down inside of me over what I see Hazel's done. Before I can suck them back in, words—hurtful words—come rushing out of my mouth.

"You stupid little brat! You had no right bothering my stuff! I hate you!"

Snatching up my papers, I throw them onto my cot fast as I can. Hazel's snubbing and sniffing over in the corner.

It's good enough for her, I think. *She ought to cry. She ought to weep and wail over what she done. Them's my things, my papers, my pencils, my crayons. She had no right! No right at all to do what she done.*

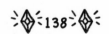

Mama said Hazel was like a delicate flower and should be handled with care. Now I don't know much about delicate flowers, but I've got the good sense to know that most of the time not far from a sweet-smelling flower is a bee circling 'round, just waiting for someone to get in its way so's it can sting the living daylights out of its unsuspecting victim. As far as I'm concerned, Hazel's not the flower right now; she's that pesky, annoying bee.

She's sobbing. I stop snatching papers and gape over my shoulder.

Crouched into a corner, her knees are pulled to her chest and her head dropped low into her lap. Her arms are wrapped tight around her knees and she's rocking back and forth.

Suddenly I'm ashamed.

Mama said since I was the oldest it was up to me to set the example for the rest. Swallowing hard, my heart breaks into tiny pieces. I wish I could suck every last one of them words back in. I fall to my knees and crawl across the wagon floor to my baby sister. I scoop her into my arms and pull her to my chest.

"Hazel, I'm sorry. I didn't mean it. You're not a brat. I just lost my temper, and I shouldn't have. Can you forgive me?"

She's sniffing, and snubbing, and jerking, trying her best to suck in air. Her face is blotchy and her eyes are as swollen and red as ripe cherries hanging from a tree. She looks me in the eyes and timidly asks, "Do you really hate me?" Then she bursts into her weeping and wailing all over again.

I hug her tighter.

"Oh, Hazel, I don't hate you. I shouldn't have said that. I was just angry because you got my things without asking."

She stops sobbing long enough to look me in the eyes again. "You promise?" she asks. "You promise you don't hate me?"

I smile and kiss her forehead. "Yes, honey, I promise. I don't hate you. I love you, very much."

She uncurls and throws her arms around my neck.

My arms wrap around her like a warm blanket.

While we're still huddled together I feel Daddy hitching up Old Stump, and I reckon he's dragging the wagon into the center of town getting ready for the show.

"Next time you want to draw with my things though, just ask, okay? All you have to do is ask."

She nods and smiles.

"All right now, Hazel, are we good? You forgive me, don't you?"

She nods again and wipes her nose with the back of her hand.

"I think we can do better than that," I say, pulling a handkerchief from under my pillow. "Blow. Now, I reckon Daddy's aiming to do a show this evening and you and I both need to be a part of it, okay?"

She nods again.

I lose her hold and stand, knowing what I need to do next. But, before I can, Hazel tugs at my dress-tail.

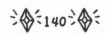

"Chestnut?"

"Yes."

"I love you."

"I love you more, you little nut!"

I turn from her, suddenly remembering my own fears.

What if someone recognizes me and calls the sheriff? I rummage through an old trunk under Mac's cot where we keep things we don't use anymore. There has to be some way to disguise myself so that when the sheriff and the store owner do come looking, they won't find me so quick.

A couple of dresses, ones I've outgrown, stored away waiting for Hazel to get bigger, pants with more holes in them than material, one glove, and . . .

Everything's on the floor of the wagon now, everything but this large brown floppy hat at the very bottom of the trunk. I don't remember this. Wonder where it came from and why—

"Chestnut! Let's go! Showtime!"

Daddy's familiar call sends a sudden chill up my backbone.

Hazel hops out first.

I swing around to the back before jumping off and walking away from my family.

Abraham starts his strumming and the triplets go to singing. Folks gather, and Daddy's flitting and flipping around, working them like they was his puppets. When the crowd's big enough, and the music's loud enough, Daddy catches my eye.

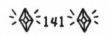

He does a double take. Must be the floppy hat. He looks at me again, then gives a nod, my cue to begin working the crowd.

I start into my speech, but out the corner of my eye I see an owner stomping out of his store with his hands on his hips, and he looks mad. His face is red and his lips are formed tight in a line. He's looking over the crowd and he's looking at Daddy. I pull the hat down tight over my eyes, but don't miss a beat of my speech. Matter of fact, I'm reciting it better than I ever have before.

Mister Abraham and the triplets are singing like nobody's business and they's money being passed to the front and bottles of elixir being passed to the back faster than a cat can lap up a bowl of milk. I'm distracted, but as soon as Daddy's sold his last bottle of elixir and Mister Abraham and the triplets are packing up getting ready to head out of town, I look back over at the store owner.

He's waving his arm through the air like he's swatting every fly in the county. Suddenly I realize he's not swatting flies though. What he's doing is flagging down the sheriff.

20

WAYWARD BOYS

D addy, please," I say, as the last of the crowd's walking away. "Please, let's leave town tonight. I can't stay here one more minute. I'm scared. I've got a bad feeling about this town. I'm just sure something's about to happen."

Daddy looks me up and down like he thinks I've lost every last bit of my mind.

"Chestnut, Abraham and I are tired. We need to get a few hours sleep before we hit the road again, and I've got an errand to run in town before we leave."

"Daddy, please. You know I've never asked anything like this before. But we've just got to get out of town tonight. Something bad is going to happen, I just know it."

Daddy looks at Abraham. He rolls his eyes and shakes his head.

Abraham shrugs. "Sometimes de children got smarts older folks don't, Slim," he says, pulling the flap down over the elixir and bolting it into place. "Sometime dey's right. Sometime dey's not. Jes' don't neber know 'bout dese things, but best to listen, I say."

The sun's low, and an eerie sort of quiet's fallen over the camp.

Daddy looks at Abraham, and then back at me. He gazes up and down the town's streets, where there's more than a few folks still stirring, then he lifts his tall black hat, scratches his head, and nods.

"All right," he says. "As long as it's all right with Abraham, I suppose it's all right with me. I've still got that errand to run, but get on up in the wagon and soon as we get things squared away, we'll hightail it out of town. Next town we come to though, I'm taking you to a doctor, girl. There's something wrong with you. I declare, Chestnut, you're acting plum peculiar, even for a nut."

"Oh, thank you, Daddy. Thank you. Now, please, hurry!"

There's still packing to do, but I run up the steps and into the wagon faster than a snake in the sunshine slithers under a rock for shade. I bolt the door, jump past the triplets, and flop back on my cot, feeling mighty fine about Daddy agreeing to something I want for a change.

"What's wrong?" Filbert asks.

"Nothing, we're just getting out of town tonight."

"Why? Daddy said he was tired."

"Don't you worry about it. We just are, that's all. Now lie down and go to sleep."

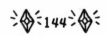

Daddy and Abraham are working around outside when suddenly, I remember my flyers. No way I can forget to put those up, especially since Hazel done what she did. Then again, how can I nail them up with the sheriff on the lookout for me?

Daddy said he had to go back into town. What if he sees me nailing up the flyers? What will he say then? Or worse, what if he reads the flyers? I mean, I want Mama to be able to find me, but I got the fear of being caught for thieving running around in my mind plus the fear of Daddy finding out what I'm doing.

I lie on my cot just a minute or two more before making my decision.

"I'll be right back," I say to the triplets—well really just to Filbert. Mac and Hazel are already breathing the rhythm of the sleeping. "Don't let Daddy leave without me."

"Chestnut, I'm telling!"

"Hush, Filbert! I'll be back before Daddy misses me. Don't say a word, all right? This is just something I've got to do."

I grab up my flyers, a handful of nails, and Daddy's hammer, and off I go through the door, out of sight of Daddy and Abraham.

The night breeze blowing in off the waters gives a welcome break from the sweltering heat of the day. Even a just-beginning woman like me gets tired of wiping sweat. After all, Mama says wiping sweat just isn't ladylike.

I run from storefront to storefront and from wooden pole to wooden pole, nailing up flyers faster than I ever have

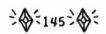

before. I don't see hide nor hair of the sheriff or the store owner, but every step I take I look over my shoulder for the both of them—and for Daddy. Running every step of the way back to the wagon, I'm hoping I can get back to my cot before Daddy's back too and notices I'm gone.

I'm almost out of the town when suddenly I see Daddy.

But he don't see me.

Least, I don't think he does. I jump behind a large grove of bottlebrush shrubs in full bloom with its spikes of bright orangey red. No way I can let Daddy know I'm here, so I stay back between the blooms, out of sight.

But, what in the world is he doing?

Still dressed in his black show suit, he walks past the Beaumont Bank and Loan, and Frannie's Fabulous Fish House, toward the end of the street, and he's not walking slow. Matter of fact you might say he's racing against himself. But where is he going, I wonder.

I stretch my neck and inch around the side of the bottle-brush for a better look. Hard to see in the darkness though. The only other building I see is a two-story on the edge of town—a beautiful white Victorian with shutters painted a washed-out cabbage sort of green and black rocking chairs lining the porch out front. I strain and squint and barely make out the sign:

BEAUMONT'S HOME FOR WAYWARD BOYS

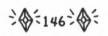

He ambles up the steps, and knocks. He don't turn around to see if anyone's looking, and I reckon by that, this isn't the first time he's done something like this. But why would he knock on *their* door?

He's set my mind to jumping with way more questions than answers. Why would he visit a home for wayward boys? Does he know someone here? What do wayward boys need with elixir? And just what in the world is a wayward boy, anyway?

The door opens slowly and an older lady with white hair and glasses steps onto the porch. Daddy shakes her hand and then I see him pull something from his pocket and give it to her. I can't rightly tell what it is, even though I'm stretching my neck and squinting my eyes like I do when I'm swimming underwater in the ponds back near the coal mines.

After just a short while, the lady dabs at her eyes with a handkerchief, and then goes back into the house. Daddy turns to leave.

I've got the good sense to know I'd better hightail it back to the wagon fast as my bony legs will carry me, but if I leave now he'll see me, no doubt.

No way I can let him know what I been up to, but I sure would like to know the same of him.

I jump back behind the bottlebrush until he's past. And still I wait. I can't start too soon for fear he'll hear me and turn around quick. Best I wait, least until he's had time to get back to camp.

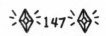

147

Sneaking in close to camp, I see Daddy working around and hitching up Old Stump. I make my way to the back of the wagon quieter than a calico stalking a blue jay. Just as I think I've got it made and got back before he spots me, "Oh!" I holler, running smack-dab into the chest of Mister Abraham.

"I's sorry. Didn' means to skeer you, missy. I thought you's in de wagon already."

"Um . . . no, Mister Abraham, but I'm going in now." I take the steps two by two. "Mister Abraham," I say, "please don't tell Daddy you saw me out of the wagon, all right?"

"I ain't sees nutin', little lady."

"Where you been?" Filbert asks, through a sleepy yawn.

"Nowhere. Now go to sleep."

I plop back on my cot and stare through the window at the night sky. It seems no time at all before the wagon rocks from side to side as Daddy and Abraham climb on board. We jerk backwards and I give a sigh, knowing we're on our way out of town and on to Houston.

But I don't sleep.

I can't, not when this gnawing, sick feeling is planted firm and growing roots in my stomach.

My mind goes back over the last few days but stops when it comes to the part where I stole the money from the store. I still can't believe I done it.

Mama says be sure your sins will find you out. Nothing left to do now but wait for that to happen.

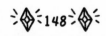

Until now, the worst thing I ever done—besides Daddy's lies, and slipping up and telling Hazel I hate her of course—is pushing Davy Johnson into Miner's Creek. But I had to do it, on account of he was pestering me, pulling my hair, and calling me names in front of the rest of the kids at school.

He called me a "slick-headed, liver-lilied shack poke" because I wouldn't let him cheat off my paper in Mrs. Warren's second-grade class.

Mama said I should have overlooked it—said sticks and stones was only thing that would hurt me and that names never would.

That's the only time I ever remember Mama being wrong, bless her heart.

Them names Davy Johnson called me did hurt. They hurt my feelings down deep. Still stick with me to this day too, and I reckon they always will.

After that, weren't nothing I could do but push him over—head first—into Miner's Creek. He screamed and whooped like he was drowning, yelling, "Help! Help! I can't swim! Somebody, save me!"

Reckon he might have drowned too, except I hollered over and told him all he had to do to save his sorry hide was stand to his feet and stop swatting at the water. Oh, he knew in his mind that water weren't deep enough to drown in, but he said he couldn't swim. He was thrashing around in there like a fish out of water. Still makes me smile to think about it today.

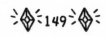

I've done loads worse than that now though and I'm not proud. But when I take that money to the train station, lay it down and buy my ticket, and get back to Mama and a loving home, I know she'll know what to do to help me set things right.

I've done a lot of thinking on it too.

What if Mama doesn't come looking for us?

Oh, it's not that she don't want to, I'm sure, it's just that she's not got the money to get on a train and go from town to town to town to find us.

And maybe she's not able.

Maybe she's so sick with worry she just clear ain't able. She probably took to her sick bed on account of the way Daddy done her—stealing her young'uns and running off with us like he done. That's all right though because I'm going to get to her sooner rather than later. I'll make it all right, you'll see. We'll get back on the train—together. She'll dress up in her prettiest dress, fix her hair like the fancy ladies in the downtown shops, and we'll come together to rescue the triplets.

Then, when he lays eyes on her, Daddy will run to meet Mama, scoop her up in his arms, and tell her how sorry he is for snatching us up and carting us off like he did.

Mama will smile and tell him, "Of course I forgive you." She'll say, "I love you, Slim Hill," and he'll say, "I love you, Mavis," right back at her.

They'll hug and kiss right there in the middle of the street with the whole town looking on. Some folks might even clap.

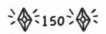

Then Daddy will wrap his arm around Mama's shoulder and grab up the triplets with the other arm. Mama will wrap one arm around Daddy's waist and the other around me. We'll walk down the street to the train station like a normal, happy family. Then, we'll all get on a train and head back to Kentucky.

Daddy will take all the money he's saved from selling elixir and buy Mama a new home, and all of us—Mama, Daddy, Filbert, Mac, Hazel, and me—will live just as happy as we can be, all the rest of our lives, right there in the hills and hollers of good old Kentucky.

And those are the thoughts I go to sleep on as Daddy and Abraham and Old Stump drive us out of this town, and far away from all the troubles that are here.

21

Gritted Teeth

The next morning, while we're camped just outside of town, somewhere between Beaumont, Texas, and Houston, it's the wind whistling through the cracks in the wagon that wakes me from my sleeping. I yawn and stretch and run my fingers through my hair.

The triplets are still sleeping the sleep of the innocent.

I say let them lie.

Stumbling out of the wagon, the first thing I see is Abraham, drinking coffee and pulling dirt and sand closer to the edges of the fire. The wind's whipping around something fierce and the sky's so dark it looks more like early evening than morning.

"Mawnin', little lady," Abraham says. "How ya'll are dis mawnin?"

"Morning, Mister Abraham. I'm okay. Where's Daddy?"

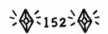

"Aw, he done goed into town," he says, reaching to pick up his banjo. "He be back soon, don't you worry." He stares at the sky and scratches at his whiskery chin with his gnarly fingers. "Hope he git back afore it storm, though."

"Looks like it might be a bad one."

"Sho' nuff do," he says. "Sho' nuff do. You wants a cup o' java, little lady?"

"Java? What's java?"

Abraham laughs. "De coffee dere," he says.

"Oh, no, thank you."

I sit across from him, cross-legged on the ground, trying to smooth the night bunnies from my hair with my fingers. I stare at Abraham, thinking what a kind face he has, but wondering why I can't remember him well from before.

"Mister Abraham? May I ask you a question?"

"Sho' nuff, little lady. Ask away."

"If you was a friend of Daddy's, how come you never came to our house?"

Abraham eyes the sky.

"I mean, it can't be on account of you're . . . well . . . because you're a . . ."

"You mean on accounts of de color o' my skin, missy?"

He smiles.

"Yes, sir. I mean, no, sir. I mean . . . well, it's not like we didn't have Negros around our house. Mister Rusko who lived about a mile from us came and helped Daddy put in a fence

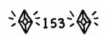

one time and Mama asked him in for lunch, but you . . . I mean . . . well, Daddy says you was his friend from the mines, but I don't ever remember you coming around."

Abraham plucks at his banjo and swallows hard. "Well now, dat do make a body wonder, don't it?" He doesn't look up from his stringing but clears his throat. "S'pose you gots a right to ask yo' question and s'pose dat question d'serve an answer. But some things . . . well . . . s'pose some questions just not that easy answer. Reckon you'd just have to ask yo' mama about dat one."

Again he starts to pluck on the strings, humming softly to the tune he's playing.

Staring off into the distance, I see the tiny town. Seems as though unless there's more that's hidden, I can see the entire town, end to end. Nice to be in a smaller town for a change.

"Mister Abraham, may I ask another question?"

"Sho' nuff, you ken, missy."

"Do you like being with us? I mean, do you like being with Daddy?"

He stops plucking, lays his banjo to the side, and pours another cup of coffee.

"Oh, yes'm. Yo' daddy a fine man." He winks and smiles and looks so convincing it almost makes me believe what he's saying.

"Why you ask dat, little lady?"

"Well, awhile back, there was a store owner acting like he thought Negros was, well, um . . ."

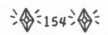

"Don't be a-skert. You ken say it to ol' Abraham. It won't hurt me none."

I swallow hard then take a deep breath.

"Well, like they was different or something."

"Some say so," Abraham says, nodding.

I look at him, sipping his coffee, rubbing his hand through his dandelion fluff hair and across the lengthening whiskers on his face. He stares way off, like he's looking into the future—or maybe even into the past. His hands are knotty and twisted, but his skin's as smooth as Hazel's.

He looks to the sky, with its fast-moving elephant-gray clouds and thunder rumbling not so far off in the distance. The wind's picking up too, whipping the tall grasses around, snapping the smallest dead branches from the trees, sending them hurling into our camp.

"Maybe I will try a cup of that coffee," I say, halfway hoping it will calm the shakiness I'm beginning to feel inside.

"Now you talkin'," he says, winking. He fetches a cup and hands it to me. I take it, gently bumping against his fingers as I put my hand around the cup. As I do I watch him, just to see his reaction.

He smiles. "You ever touched a Negro, little lady?" he asks softly.

I shake my head and stare at the ground, feeling my face turn all the hot, steamy reds of embarrassment at the thought of him knowing what I done and why.

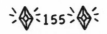

"What you think?" he asks. "Do it feel different from yours?"

"No, sir," I say, glancing at him then looking away quickly.

We sit together without talking, the wind swirling and the sky growing darker by the minute.

"So, why all the fuss, Mister Abraham—about keeping Negros and whites apart, I mean? If we're the same except for the color of our skin, why do folk make such a ruckus?"

"Can't rightly say, missy. Maybe someday it be different, but not now."

He picks up a long stick and scratches around in the fire, then clears his throat to speak, his voice quiet.

"Now den, ken I's ask you a question, little lady?" He takes another sip of his coffee.

"Yes, sir." I place the coffee he's poured for me to my lips but don't sip, the smell of it bitter and unpleasant.

"What you got ag'in your daddy?"

"Sir?"

"I means, why you don't like him?"

Abraham's question is like a wet slap in the face, and I lose my breath for a second at the thought of it. No way I can tell him how I really feel; then again, it seems he already knows.

"It's not that I don't like him, Mister Abraham—it's that he don't like me. I mean, he's nice to the triplets and all loving on them, but he don't act like he wants to be around me, always making me walk ahead or lag behind the rest of the family like he does. It's like he's ashamed to have me around."

Abraham sips his coffee. "Ain't dat easy."

"Sir?"

"Ain't dat easy for a man and a growin' girl. Yo' daddy want to love you, but he got his own demons."

"Demons? You mean he's possessed with the devil, Mister Abraham?"

Abraham laughs a warm, hearty laugh that makes me feel comfortable in his presence.

"I mean he still think about yo' mama and how she done him. He know you feel hard at him for dat. Reckon he don't forgive himself for de way he hurt you."

I set the coffee cup on the ground in front of the fire.

"Mister Abraham, you're talking in riddles. Mama didn't do nothing. It was Daddy who stole us away. Mama went to town, and while she was in the store, Daddy run off with us."

"You sure 'bout dat?" Abraham asks with raised eyebrows and more questions than answers on his face.

"Well yes, sir; I was there."

"Maybe you was, but things not always de way dey seem. You think about dat, missy. Jes' you think. Dat's all ol' Abraham say."

I look into the fire and grit my teeth. What does he know? The only information he has is wrapped up in the lies Daddy's told him. He wasn't there, I was, and if Daddy feels bad . . . well . . . I reckon maybe he should.

The triplets stumble from the wagon, practically falling on top of each other.

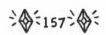

Mac comes out last and stays back, on the top step of the wagon. He's looking around like he's trying his best to figure out where in the world he is. He rubs his eyes and squints, leaning out for a closer look. He scratches his head and his chin falls to his chest like maybe he's just seen a ghost floating by.

"What's that?" he asks, pointing off in the distance, where the grass reaches up to touch the sky.

Abraham jumps to his feet kicking dirt into the fire, grabs his banjo, and runs with it to the wagon. He places it inside, then grabs Hazel and Mac by the hand.

"Git de udder boy!" he yells to me, wagging his finger toward Filbert. "Follow me, quick!"

Abraham sprints toward town, with Hazel on one side and Mac on the other.

Hazel, the look of a bear caught in a trap on her face, stares back at me and begins to cry. I shake my head "no" but it don't help. In an instant her face is as red as a strawberry and tears run the length of her round dimpled cheeks.

Mac shoves his hand deep into his pocket. As wild-eyed as I've ever seen him, he looks around like he's expecting to be snatched up at any second by a giant bird and be carried off by his earlobes to another country.

Filbert and I follow close behind. I don't know where we're going or why, and I sure don't know where my daddy is, but I got a sneaky feeling it's best to do what Abraham

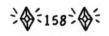

says right now, especially since Abraham's not prone to excitability.

Though the town clock would argue, it's not daytime anymore, and the winds are moving in and circling like a smoky ring. And worse, it's beginning to rain.

"Chestnut, what's happening?" Filbert asks. I hear the fear in his voice and for once I decide that his question is one I'd rather not answer.

Abraham snatches a look over his shoulder, and all I can make of it is the panic in his eyes. Without a word, he scoops up Hazel and plops her on his shoulders, then grabs Mac by the hand again and races on, faster than before. From the look he sees on Abraham's face, I reckon Mac knows to run as fast as he can, and I pick up my pace, too. I don't know what we're runnin' from, but no way I'm looking back. No way I want to risk being turned into a pillar of salt, like Mister Lot's wife in the Bible.

"Run, Filbert, run!" I holler grabbing to his hand, but I'm not sure he hears me above the roar of the winds that practically pick us up and sweep us down the street.

Abraham's far ahead now, farther ahead than he would be if it was just me following after him. He disappears from sight, but when we get closer, I can see that he's ducked into a store. Least, I reckon it's a store; the sign out front is swinging so fast and smacking against the bricks so hard that I can't make out the letters.

The rain's mixing with hail and slapping me and Filbert in the face. We duck into the building after them, to find Abraham hollering, "Git out de way o' de windows! Git back! Git back!"

There's not but the five of us and two other folk in the store—two ladies—and they're looking at Abraham with their mouths gaped open, like he's a criminal that steals young'uns like us. But with Hazel still perched on his shoulders and Mac at his side, Abraham don't seem to pay them no mind.

"Twister!" he yells. "Comin' dis way! Git down! Git down!"

Just about the time those words come spewing from his mouth, the plate glass window in front of the store shatters into at least a million tiny pieces, sending glass flying through the air like a hawk in chase of a rabbit. One end of a park bench comes barreling through the opening.

The ladies scream.

At the back of the store, I scooch up next to Filbert and cover his head with mine, turning my face away from the tiny pieces of glass flying through the air.

Abraham does the same with Hazel and Mac, and he slings an outstretched arm over my shoulders too.

The store ladies huddle together and by the way their shoulders are rising and falling, they're the ones doing the sobbing.

The way I've got it figured—this is the day the lot of us will come face to face with our Maker.

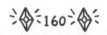

22

RUNNING LIKE THE WIND

I've never heard such a racket in my life.

Stuff is falling off shelves, flying through the air like mad blue jays fighting to keep a calico from their nest. And the wind so loud, can't hear nothing but the sound of that train engine roaring through my head.

But, as sudden as it come, it's gone.

The two ladies in back of the store un-huddle and chase each other to the front, to stare out over the breakings.

"Chestnut, what . . . what . . . what was that?" Filbert asks.

"Twister, I reckon," I say, picking glass from his hair and looking him head to toe for cuts and bruises.

"Ya'll all right?" Abraham asks, helping Hazel and Mac to their feet.

"Wow!" says Filbert, pulling from my grip and running to the front of the store. "That was great! Is another one coming?"

Abraham's got Hazel and Mac by the hand and is on his way to the door, not turning to answer Filbert.

Those two store ladies must have got ahold of their selves right quick, because as we are walking from the store one of them says, right out loud for us to hear, "That's just not proper! What's a Negro man doing holding tight to four little white children?"

Abraham?

He doesn't say a word.

He just nods, smiles, and keeps on walking.

The second lady opens her mouth and her words come flying to my ears. "He ought to be reported to the sheriff," she says. "I'll bet he wouldn't be so quick to hold those children by the hand if he knew the law was aware of what he was doing."

All of a sudden something I can't control takes over my mind. And my mouth. I stop in my tracks, right there in the middle of the store, throw my hands on my hips, and square off with the second lady who's done the talking.

"I'll tell you what he's doing," I say, without a hesitation. "He's saving our lives, that's what he's doing! We got trouble and our daddy's nowhere to be found, but Mister Abraham here saved our hides!"

"Well!" the lady huffed, but she didn't say anything else.

Now that it's over and done, I am sorry for talking back to my elder. Reckon Mama would be fierce disappointed if she'd heard, but I'm not sorry for what I said. Those ladies

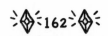

are way too high and mighty for their own good, and I reckon a backwoods country gal like me can set them on the straight and narrow.

Still, I'm so regretful for my rudeness that I stop again and turn around to face the ladies. "I'm sorry if what I said was hurtful, ma'am. I didn't mean no disrespect." And I turn again to go.

Following Abraham from the store, Filbert and me run smack dab into the sheriff. Not the Beaumont sheriff, but the sheriff of this town we're in now.

Soon as I see that star on his shirt, I turn, hang my head, and try best as I can to hide my face in my dress. I think at first he's come to check on the store owners and the damage. But soon as he looks me up and down, like he's wondering if I'm the one he's looking for, I'm in a tizzy all over again.

I lay hold to the first triplet I come to, pulling Mac close, bending over like I'm looking through his hair for glass. And then as soon as the sheriff turns away, I take off running back down the street toward the wagon, dragging Mac behind me.

"Chestnut? Why are we running?" Mac yells. "Is there another twister coming?"

"Just hurry," I say.

First thing we see is Old Stump, still tied beside the tree right where we left her. She looks sort of wild out of her eyes too, like she's wondering what in the world has happened, but there's not one scratch on her hide that wasn't there already.

And our wagon?

Well, our poor wagon hasn't fared nearly so well. It's flipped on its side—the side where Daddy stores the elixir—and it seems to me there's elixir pouring out all over the ground, mixing in with the dirt.

Suddenly, from out of nowhere it seems, Daddy comes running. He's out of breath and panting like a dog fresh off the hunt for a rabbit or even a pheasant or two.

"Abraham! Abraham!" he yells, as he comes closer. "Chestnut, is everyone all right?"

"We's good, Slim," Abraham yells back. "We's all fine here!"

When Daddy reaches the wagon, he grabs hold to the triplets first thing. Then he slaps Abraham on the back, not even noticing I'm around.

"I saw it first, Daddy!" says Mac. "I saw it coming across the way!"

"Yeah," Filbert chimes in, "then Abraham snatched them up and run into town, to the store. Me and Chestnut ran along behind."

"And the windows all broke, and glass went everywhere," says Hazel. "But I wasn't scared, Daddy, not at all!"

Abraham rubs his forehead with his sleeve and looks at Daddy and winks. He lets out a long breath.

"Oh, my goodness," Daddy says. "I'm sorry I wasn't here, but thanks to you, Abraham, my children are alive. I owe you my life, my friend." He shakes Abraham's hand, then slaps him hard on the back.

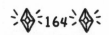

"Well, deys nothin' hurt but de wagon, and prob'ly de elixir," Abraham says, rubbing the side of the wagon with his hands. "Lookin' like we gots ourselves a mess."

Daddy scratches his head, squats low, and tries his best to see under the wagon.

"From the looks of the broken glass and the liquid pooled under the wagon, I'd say we've lost the elixir, or most of it anyway. Then again, really no way to tell until we right the wagon. We did get an awful lot of rain, so it might just be puddled water." Daddy walks around and around the wagon, inspecting every inch of it for damage. "It'll take all of us plus Old Stump to get the wagon upright and back on her wheels again."

"Don't worry, Daddy," Filbert says. "We can do it! We can lift the wagon. You'll see. I'm strong!"

"I'm stronger," Mac yells.

"But not as strong as me," hollers Hazel, above the both of them.

Daddy looks to Abraham and smiles. "Well then, I say no time like the present to put that strength to work! Let's get to it."

The rest of the day we work, righting the wagon, cleaning the mess of broken elixir bottles, and tidying up the inside. All in all, Daddy lost close to one hundred bottles, but to my surprise he isn't awfully upset. But he does surprise me with somethin' else.

"What's this?" Daddy asks, and he reaches down and picks up a piece of soggy paper that had blown under the bushes.

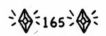

I swallow hard, realizing right away what's in his hand. "Um, it's . . . um . . ."

"Chestnut, are these yours?"

23

I Got Dreams

"Are these pictures yours, Chestnut?" Daddy asks again. I don't see any way out of this but the truth.

"Um, yes, sir."

"You draw them?"

"Yes, sir."

"They're nice. I like the way you've drawn the wagon. Looks . . . real."

I need to sit. Daddy's not paid me a compliment in as long as I can remember. Matter of fact, he don't even know me well enough to pay me a compliment. Not really, not like a father ought to know his firstborn, that is. He doesn't know my dreams, or my wants, so him saying something nice to me comes as a huge surprise.

"What are you planning to do with this talent of yours?" Daddy asks looking from the flyers to me and then back to the flyers again.

"I-I-I don't understand," I say, wondering if he's on to me. Does he know what my flyers are for? "What do you mean what am I going to do with it?"

"Chestnut's gonna do same as you when she grows up, Daddy," Mac says. "She's gonna sell elixir and get rich."

Mac's crawling around on the ground around the wagon.

"Am not!" I say, puffing out my chest and feeling sort of proud I've told Daddy I've no intention of following in his footsteps.

"I know what Chestnut's gonna do," says Filbert. "She's gonna get married and have bunches and bunches of babies, like Hazel."

"I'm not a baby!" Hazel yells, slapping Filbert on the arm.

Filbert takes off running with Hazel close behind.

Filbert's's got me thinking. What if I did decide I wanted a happy home with a husband and young'uns in the yard? What if my husband up and run off with my young'uns, like Daddy did with us? Where would I be then?

I tell you where I'd be.

I'd be same place as Mama is now: pining away, crying my eyeballs out, searching the hills and hollers day and night for some no-good man who didn't love me enough to stay and keep the home fires burning. Or worse, lying flat on my back in my sick bed, sick with worry over my young'uns.

Not me.

That kind of life's not what I'm aiming for.

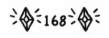

168

"All right, you two. Stop teasing your sister," Daddy says, interrupting my thoughts. "Abraham, let's see if maybe we can salvage some of these bottles, at least the ones that aren't too badly damaged."

And just like that, Daddy's mind is off me and back on him and making his money.

How I wish he would talk to me long enough to know that my dream is to go to . . . oh, say, Paris, France, and study drawing and painting in one of those fancy-schmancy art schools Mama told me about.

And I want to spend my days sitting beside the cornflower blue sea, with foamy waves slapping at my legs, the lemon yellow sunshine beating down on my back, and seagulls swooping down around me, sucking up all the tiny fish they can hold in their beaks.

I want to sit up to my waist in the ocean, with a paintbrush in my hand and all the watercolors of the rainbow circling around me. I want to paint all the blues in the sky and the whites and grays of the ocean waves that race to get to the shore.

I want to throw away my shoes with the holes in the bottoms and dig down into the lamb's wool–colored sand with my toes. Then I'd let the warm, salty water of the ocean wash them clean again. I want to—

"Chestnut? Chestnut? Did you hear me?"

"Um, no, sir. Sorry."

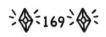

"Girl, are you daydreaming again? I said what are you planning on doing with these? There's so many, and they're all of the same thing, the wagon and Old Stump's rear." He shuffles through them like he's expecting the picture to suddenly change.

I stand on my tiptoes and look over his shoulder, sick with worry over what I'll find. I let out a long sigh. Those flyers he's got in his hands don't have any writing on them. That means he still hasn't got a clue what I'm doing. I didn't even remember keeping those flyers; they were the first ones I did.

I've never in my life been so happy that I didn't finish something. Until this minute, I was always angry when Daddy called me a procrastinator. Not anymore. Matter of fact from now on I'm going to wear that word around my neck, like a medal.

"They're all wet and soggy now. Why don't we just throw these away?"

I grab them from him. "No, sir," I say. "I want to save them. I need them for a . . . a . . . a pattern! Yes, that's right, a pattern, so's I can draw more."

"Well, all right, but I can't for the life of me see why you would need so many pictures that all look alike. Take them and put them away inside the wagon."

"Yes, sir," I say, pulling the papers to my chest, sloshing in mud to my ankles to the back of the wagon.

Hazel, on her knees near the backside of the wagon, her green cotton ragbag dress wet and soppy and as muddy as

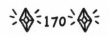

I've ever known it to be, is tugging and pulling at something. She mumbles to herself as she tugs.

"Hazel, what are you doing crawling around in the mud?" I ask.

"I found . . . this . . . box . . . and I'm trying to pull . . . it . . . out . . ."

She rips my metal box from the mud and lifts the lid in one smooth motion.

"Hazel, don't!" I jump toward her just in time to slam the lid on the box.

But not before she lays eyes to the money and gasps. "Chestnut? Where did you get all that money?"

24

CAUGHT

Hazel's eyes are as big as pumpkins.

"I never seen so much—"

"It's none of your beeswax so never you mind," I say, jerking the box from her hands and pulling it to my chest.

"Daddy, Chestnut gots—"

"Stop it!" I say, shoving my flyers up under my arm and covering Hazel's mouth with my hand. I grit my teeth and get down next to her ear. "If you tell, I promise you'll be sorry!"

"That's enough," Daddy says, rounding the back of the wagon with his arms full of rescued elixir bottles. "Leave Chestnut alone, Hazel. When you get to be her age, you can have secrets too. Now into the wagon, young'uns! Abraham, let's be on our way. We've salvaged all we can here. I'll go into the next town we come to and buy some more bottles."

"Dat's fine!" Abraham says. "De wagon and Old Stump, dey both be's ready to go."

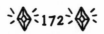

Inside the wagon I rub my box clean with my hands. "Hazel, I think I heard Daddy calling you," I say, pointing to the wagon's door with a nod of my head. As soon as she looks away, I place my box back under my cot and shove it back to the wall.

Hazel turns back to me and sheepishly eyes me like the mouse that got away from the cat.

"If you bother my stuff again, I'll let you have it," I say, balling up my fist and showing it to her.

She sticks out her tongue. Still very much a baby, she's every bit as sly and manipulative at seven as any adult would be, especially an adult like Daddy. If she's got something on her mind you can bet your bottom dollar it'll come out of her mouth before too long.

"So, where did you get it?" she asks, approaching me slowly and planting herself like a tree on the bottom of my cot.

"Hazel, just don't worry about it, all right?"

I turn away, hoping she'll wander back to her own space. I should know better.

"But they's millions and millions of dollars in there!"

"Shh! And there is not millions, Hazel."

"What's going on?" Filbert asks, flopping back on his cot with his Babe Ruth picture book.

"Nothing's going on," I snap. "Just Hazel making up tales again."

Hazel gasps.

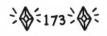

"Aw, Chestnut, I'm telling!"

"Just shush, and I mean it. There's not that much money in there, leastwise not as much as you think, so just forget it. Anyway, Daddy tells fibs, so I can too."

"Daddy don't fib. Everything he says is truth," Mac says.

I do what I can to get their minds—especially Hazel's—off my things. For the next three weeks we bump along dry, dusty roads, watching nothing go by us but flat land. Daddy likes to take his time and set up camp at every pretty patch along the road that we come to.

While we ride, I draw, and I dream of having fancy paints and canvases like the ones Mama showed me in her Sears catalog. I dream of having Mama close again.

Late one evening, about the time I'm ready to turn in for the night to do some serious sleeping, Daddy hollers, "There she is! Houston, Texas, here we come!"

Tired as I am, I've never been so happy to hear Daddy shout out a town in all my born days.

Hazel and Mac jump to the front of the wagon and lean out the door over Daddy's shoulder, taking in the sights. But it's night, and we're on the outskirts of town. Little do those two know, there's not much to be seen from here but twinkly lights.

"So, where did you get the money?" Filbert asks, balancing his book on his stomach like a circus performer.

"How come you're asking me about that now?" I say, lying back on my cot and breathing deep, worried that what he's heard is still weighing heavy on his mind after all this time.

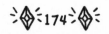

"Anyway, it's not that much," I say. "You know how Hazel stretches things."

I look away but hear Filbert grunt, "Humph!" Just like Daddy.

In the late afternoon of the next day, Daddy rolls the wagon into the middle of town and we do a show. Right good one too. Matter of fact, best show we've done since Abraham's been with us.

But with the bottles of elixir we lost in the tornado and the bottles we sold in the show today, Daddy says we're off about two hundred bottles.

"All right, young'uns, you know what to do. We've got to get the wagon full of elixir and that means filling up bottles—lots and lots of bottles. I'm going into town to find us some more empties, and I've got some other things I need to get done, but I'll be back soon. The three of you pull up grass and tear it tiny, tiny, tiny, so folks will think it's herbs," he says to the triplets. "Chestnut, you find water and fill the buckets to the brim. Abraham and I will do the mixing soon as I get back."

"I git de fire started," Abraham says.

I fill the wooden bucket to the brim with water and look on as the triplets shred the grass they've pulled. Soon as they're finished, off they go to gather more grass.

Daddy's gone longer than he should be just for buying bottles. Abraham must have thought it too, because right out of the blue he starts in trying to comfort me.

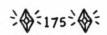

"Yo' daddy be back soon," he says. "Gonna git some food stirred up so's we can eat when he come. De day fast comin' to a close." He eyes the sky.

Pulling four small potatoes from a box under the front seat of the wagon, he takes out his pocket knife and begins to peel. He tosses the peelings into a large wrought iron skillet, popping hot with the remnants of fatback grease. He tosses the peeled potatoes into the black iron pot of boiling water, hanging over the fire.

Even though there's a gnawing in my gut for food, I've not got my mind on eating, or elixir mixing, or Daddy's being gone too long. My mind is on that money I stole, and on getting to the train station before Daddy can find out my plan or before the sheriff puts me under the jail. And before this night is over I've got more flyers to nail up, telling Mama—if she's searching—where we'll be.

"Why do you reckon Daddy goes off and leaves us like he does, Mister Abraham?"

"Don't know. Bizness, I s'pose. Maybe he busy helpin' out de orphans."

"Orphans? What orphans?" I laugh, thinking Abraham's cracking a joke. I can see by his face though, he isn't. "What are you talking about, Mister Abraham?"

"Well now, seems yo' daddy, he ain't told you ev'rything." Abraham gives me a wink and stirs up the fire with a long stick. "You know, missy, yo' daddy a good man and he sho'

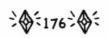

do love all ya'll. If you don't mind me sayin, ol' Abraham think he don't deserve de treatment you give him."

I stare into the fire wondering what in the world Abraham is talking about. Oh, I understand the part about Daddy not deserving the treatment I give him, but what does he mean, "business" and "the orphans"?

"Mister Abraham, I don't understand," I say after I've thought on his words for a while. "What have orphans got to do with us?"

25

THE BUSINESS WITH ORPHANS

Abraham doesn't hesitate. Instead, he seems happy to be spouting out the information he knows about my daddy.

"Well now, I bet you don't know yo' daddy give money to orphan childrens in ev'ry town he in, do you?"

I shake my head. Abraham's lost his mind.

"And I bet you don't know yo' daddy slip money in some of de hands of de older folks dat come to de show when no one lookin', do you?"

Now I know he's talking foolish. All I've ever seen Daddy do is laugh and make goo-goo eyes at the ladies. Then again, now that I think about it, the ladies are of the older variety, and he does sometimes take their hands in his, but Abraham must be mistaken. Daddy's just working the crowd, drawing them in so's he can sell more elixir. He would never just hand someone money. That's not like my daddy at all.

"But, what do the widows have to do with anything? I mean that don't even—"

"Now hold on a minute, little missy, and I'll tells you," Abraham interrupted with a wave of his hand. "Yo' daddy know you children gots all you need, so he gives de rest of his monies away. You know, Miss Ches'nut, you all gots a heap more dan any dem children in dem orphan homes gots, so yo' daddy help give dem what he never did have."

I jump to my feet. "I don't believe you. That don't sound like Daddy. Not the daddy I know. You're lying, Mister Abraham."

"Now, missy, don't git yo' dander up. It is yo' daddy, but he don't want ya'll to know."

"But that just don't make sense. Look at this!" I jerk my shoe off and shove it toward Abraham. "Just look! We're his children and we have to get our clothes from missionaries' ragbags and wear shoes with more holes than soles! Most of the time, we don't even have enough food in our stomachs to make it through the day. Why, I've had more wish meals in my life than I can count and I'm sick of living this way."

My heart wants to bust into tears but my head says don't do it. Matter of fact, if I was to cry right now it would be from the anger of it all and not from the hurt.

Surely Mister Abraham is talking about someone else's family.

Surely he don't mean mine.

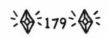

I *want* to hold my tongue, but my mouth just won't let it happen. Before I know it I'm spewing out words even I can't believe I'm saying.

"Do you know what a wish meal is, Mister Abraham?"

I don't give him time to answer. Matter of fact, I don't hardly even take a breath.

"Well, I'll tell you what a wish meal is." I plant my hands square on my hips and shake my finger in the air. "It's when your stomach aches for a bite of something—anything—but when you sit down to eat there's nothing, not a crumb or a smidgeon or even a smell there, and all you get to do is *wish* you had a meal to go in your belly."

"I know dat, missy, but dem orphan childrens gots even less dan you, don't you see? You gots a roof over yo' head, a family, and a daddy dat love you, and yo' daddy ain't gonna let you starve. Dem children ain't got none o' dat."

I bury my head in my hands, still not believing what I'm hearing.

"Anyway, yo' daddy say he don't want his children raised up proud and haughty. Ever'body know the Good Book say right before de fall come some pride, and yo' daddy, he want to raise children dats thankful for what dey got. He say dem dats gots too much ain't thankful for what dey do have. And, missy, if you'll 'scuse me for sayin' it, I think yo' daddy be right. After all, dey's sometin' else you didn't yet know. Yo' daddy and ol' Abraham was raised up together in an orphanage. Our town was so small dey only had de one home for childrens without folks. Yo' daddy bein' white growed up in de front rooms of dat orphans home, and ol' Abraham growed up in the back rooms with de other childrens like me. So I knows yo' daddy be right. Yo' daddy, he chose de right way and don't you forget it neither."

He waves his hands in the air, like he's frustrated with the things he's already said.

"Mister Abraham, I don't—"

"Now I done say too much, missy, and don't you let on like I told you, neither." He comes close, bends over, and looks me right in the eyes. "You jes' remember what ol' Abraham say. Yo' daddy, he a good, good man."

I shove my holey shoe back on my foot and stomp away.

No way I'm going to believe what Abraham is telling me about Daddy.

No way Daddy's got that big a heart in him, caring for them that don't have so much.

Huh! What kind of respectable man would let his children wear hand-me-down clothes and raggedy shoes while giving his money away? That just don't make sense. And Mama says if it don't make sense, it just ain't so. Everyone knows adults stick together like warts on the back of an old toad.

Still, now Abraham's buried a doubt seed deep in my mind.

What if . . .

Naw, it can't be so.

But, I did see him at that wayward boys home in . . .

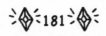

Naw. Get it out of your mind, Chestnut Hill.

I stare up into the sky. It'll be dark soon and even though I've way more questions than answers, still I've got work that needs to be done. I run into the wagon for my flyers, Daddy's hammer, and some nails. If I hurry, I can be back before Daddy knows I'm gone. I leave when Abraham's back is turned as he tends to the fire and the triplets are busy fighting over Mac's yo-yo.

Running through town, I nail flyers to every post and tree I come to. Just as I'm nailing the last flyer to a pole, a street light flickers on, and I duck, then squint, feared there's something in it going to spew out all over me at any second.

Suddenly, I feel a finger tap me on the shoulder from behind and I gasp.

"Excuse me, young lady."

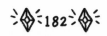

26

SECRETS AND LIES

The stranger's puffing a big smelly cigar that nearly takes my breath away. He glances at me, then back up at the light. "You ever seen electric street lights?" he asks, smoke circling his head like a kingly crown.

I shake my head, and—knowing Mama would say it wouldn't be neighborly not to speak when spoken to—I reply. "No, sir. We don't have anything like that back in Kentucky. Folks want lights, they burn a candle."

He chuckles. "I figured as much the way you were staring."

He pushes his derby to the back of his head with one finger; with the others, he flicks the ash from his cigar. He's got the biggest, roundest belly I ever did see, and I wonder how he sees over it to tie his shoes.

"It's not any of my business, little lady," he says, interrupting my thinking on his belly and his shoes, "but you shouldn't

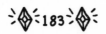

be here. This is not a proper neighborhood for a young girl after the sun goes down."

I look him up and down, and then stretch my neck to look around him at the building behind, where there's loud music spilling to the outside. Through the open doors I can see folk dancing and laughing.

"What's in there?"

He ignores my question. "What are you doing here anyway? And where are your parents?" He looks up and down the street, like he's searching for my folks.

"You ain't no runaway are you?"

I don't say anything.

His stares make me more than a tad uncomfortable, and suddenly I remember my daddy told me not to talk to strangers.

"I believe you are," he says, lifting his hat and scratching his head. "You are a runaway, aren't you? Sheriff! Sheriff!" he yells, waving his hand in the air and looking up the street toward the middle of town.

I snatch a look behind me, and then take off running toward camp. No way I want an encounter with the law.

With most of my flyers already nailed, I run as fast as my legs will go. When I get back to the wagon, Daddy's there. He took over the cooking from Abraham and there's a few boiled potatoes and a wrought iron skillet full of corn bread by the fire. The triplets are shoving food into their mouths almost as fast as if they were in an eating contest of some sort.

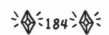

"Chestnut, where have you been?" Daddy asks. "And what are you doing with my hammer?"

"Um . . . I'm . . . well, I went back into town to look for you since you'd been gone so long, and I took this hammer to protect myself. That's what I done."

I hang my head, but not before giving a glance toward Abraham who's standing, staring at the fire, and shaking his head. He wipes his face with his hands.

I hate lying to Daddy. I hate that Abraham knows I'm lying.

I hate lying, period.

Mama would never stand for it, not even if there was a good reason for the lie. I wish there was a way to suck the lies back in, but there's not. There's no way I can look Daddy in the eyes now, even though he's the one that taught me how to lie in the first place.

"Well, I'm here now, so you can stop your looking," Daddy says. "Come sit by the fire and grab a bite to eat. We'll work on the bottles later. And do something with that hammer, will you? You're making me nervous."

Abraham's a better cook than Daddy, though I would never say it out loud. But, same as always, there's not near enough to fill a growing girl's stomach. The triplets' bellies come first; what's left is divided among the rest of us. There's no use in asking for more. There's never more in the pot.

"All right, let's get a move on," Daddy says, moving the boxes of empty bottles closer to the fire. "Chestnut, get the water bucket."

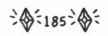

"Here's the grass, Daddy," Filbert says. "We broke it into tiny pieces, just the same as always."

"Good job! Abraham, you get the silver flask please. You know where I keep it."

"Sho' nuff."

Before we start filling the bottles, Daddy sends the triplets to bed. They protest, especially Hazel, but as usual, it doesn't work with Daddy. One thing he believes in is an early bedtime for his babies.

Once they're in bed, and the ruckus settles down, I begin filling the bottles with water.

Abraham pushes in the tiny blades of grass, and Daddy adds one dropperful of the liquid from his flask with the small medicine dropper he got from a pharmacy back in Kentucky.

Most folks back home kept spirits in their flasks. Not Daddy. He don't believe in liquor or strong drink of any kind. Says he don't want to put anything in his body that might cloud his thinking, so all he keeps in his silver flask is oil. While we work, Abraham hums. Daddy smiles, and I do my best to think.

Suddenly and quietly, a man steps into camp from the shadows.

First thing I notice are his shoes; big as rowboats in a puddle, but shinier than anything I've seen. It's clear he's wearing a uniform, and there's a gun strapped tight around his waist.

Next thing I look for is the star on his shirt. I knew it, a lawman plain as day.

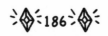

I swallow hard, knowing I'll be in jail before the moon winks twice at the night sky.

"Evening, officer," Daddy says, rising to his feet. His Adam's apple rises and falls as he speaks.

I stand, my shoulders slumped and my head hung low, expecting to be arrested for thieving and, who knows, maybe lying too.

"Chestnut, sit!" Daddy says, without turning to look at me.

"What can I do for you, sir?" Daddy asks.

"You head of this elixir outfit?" the sheriff asks, snarling when he says it and straining to look around the camp.

"Yes, sir," Daddy says, shoving a hand toward the sheriff. "Slim Hill. Proud to make your acquaintance."

The sheriff don't shake Daddy's hand but instead stares Daddy up and down, with one hand on his hip, the other on his gun.

Daddy's come to life, already pretending to be something he's not. I suspect before much longer he'll be bouncing up and down on his toes, breathing deep, and puffing out his chest.

The sheriff clears his throat and gives the camp a look-see again, stopping a bit when he lays eyes to Abraham.

"Mister Hill, you ever been to Beaumont, Texas?" the sheriff says. He's calm, but he's looking at Daddy with suspicion in his eyes.

My stomach flops like a fish on dry land.

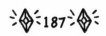
187

"Yes, sir, we were there not too long ago. Why do you ask?"

The sheriff rubs his hand across his chin. "I'll know more after I return a call from the sheriff over in Beaumont. He left a message for me today. It seems there was some money missing from a store and the owner's making accusations."

The sheriff don't take his eyes off of Daddy and it's clear that before he even hears from the sheriff in Beaumont, he's not going to believe a word Daddy says.

My heart is beating into my throat and I'm practically gasping just to take in air.

"I'll wait until I talk with him, but it would be wise for you folks to stay put, you hear?"

The sheriff raises his eyebrows and gives a nod to Abraham, like he's asking him to make sure Daddy stays put and don't leave town.

"All right, officer, and thank you," Daddy says, his eyes turned down and fixed on the ground.

Daddy's face is as white as a ghost in the light of a full moon. Shaky, he lowers himself to a sitting position on a large hollow tree stump. He pulls his hanky from his back pocket and wipes the sweat beads from his face and neck.

With the sheriff disappearing back into the shadows, Abraham speaks softly, wrapping both hands around his coffee cup.

"What we gonna do, Slim?"

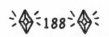

"I tell you what we're gonna do, Abraham," Daddy says without hesitation, jumping to his feet, slinging elixir bottles into boxes. "We're getting out of here is what we're gonna do."

Daddy's hands are shaking, and it seems it's all he can do to get the elixir bottles into the box rather than dropping them to the ground.

"I haven't a clue what that sheriff is talking about, but I'm not sticking around to find out. This isn't the first time a traveling salesman's being accused of something he didn't do."

It don't seem like Daddy's even taking a breath his words are coming so fast and loud, and his eyes are as wide as a moon when it's full. He's flitting around the camp faster than the triplets after a sugary sucker and sliding boxes of elixir into the wagon so fast even Old Stump looks antsy.

"Chestnut, get in the wagon and lock the door. We're going to move as fast as Old Stump can run." He plops a box of elixir bottles into Abraham's arms. "Abraham, toss this stuff and those boxes over in the wagon while I hitch her up. We'll be out of here in a flash. If we're gone when he gets back, we're as good as free. There's no way he'll know where we're headed."

I toss out the water still left in the buckets, skedaddle up the steps and into the back of the wagon, like Daddy says. My knees are sounding more like hammers tapping on a nail head than trembling bones.

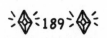

The triplets are asleep and I'm glad. No use them knowing what's going on; that one of us is about to be thrown into a cold, wet jail cell or worse, hung over a tree to swing. Best to just leave them alone and let them lie.

I fall back on my cot just as Old Stump jerks the wagon. I hear Daddy and Abraham talking fast as lightning on the wooden seat up front, but I can't make out the words.

Daddy's got Old Stump moving at such a fast pace the wind's roaring through the cracks in the wagon. I can feel every bump and rock and stump on the road, and I don't mind saying it.

I'm scared.

27

GOTCHA!

I ought to tell Daddy what I done, that I stole that money and it's me the lawman's after. Preacher back in Kentucky says confessing your sins is like a dose of medicine for the soul. Then again, if I tell Daddy, it won't be medicine that I'll need. It'll be a deep, dark burying hole.

I fall asleep worrying about the law being after us, Daddy finding out the truth, and not being able to get back to Mama. I never used to worry, but since I done so much wrong and broke so many of them commandments, I'm more afraid of meeting my Maker than of squaring off on some street corner with some sheriff. Reckon wrongdoing tends to make a body as jumpy as a one-legged chicken on a bed of hot coals.

By late in the morning we're mighty close to Dallas. Daddy's nowhere to be found and the triplets is off and playing on their own.

I stumble down the steps of the wagon, rubbing my neck. Must have slept wrong, because it's aching something fierce.

"Mornin', missy!" Abraham shouts.

There's coffee in the pot on the fire and I can smell biscuits in the Dutch oven buried up to its neck in the fire.

I breathe in deep. "Morning, Mister Abraham. Where's Daddy?"

"Oh, I 'spect he'll be along d'rectly."

I lean against the side of the wagon with my arms crossed and my conscience eating away at my soul.

"Mister Abraham, did you really mean what you said about Daddy giving money to the orphans and widows?"

"Sho' nuff did, missy. Yor daddy, he a good man, a mighty good man." Abraham gives me a wink and a nod. "Why you scratch yo' head like you don't believe?"

Abraham lifts the lid on the Dutch oven, checking the biscuits and then pours himself another cup of coffee. "Go on," he says, "tell ol' Abraham why yo' daddy want to take you away if all was so nice."

I squat, pick up a stick, and scratch in the dirt.

"I ain't rightly sure," I say shrugging, and thinking back. "I mean, Mama seemed happy, Daddy too, but the morning we all went into town together they'd had a fuss."

I squint and stare off into the distance.

"They never did too much angry jawing in front of us. Mostly went up on the hill behind the house for that."

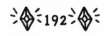

"You want some coffee?" Abraham asks, holding up a cup and the pot of coffee.

I shake my head and continue. "We'd had breakfast that morning, biscuits almost as round as plates. So big and fluffy Mama called them cat heads, and, boy oh boy, I can taste them now; right out of the wood stove with melted butter slathered all over them and sourwood honey drizzled over top. Mama's cooking couldn't be beat!"

"S'pose yor mama's biscuits make two o' dese, huh?" He lifts the lid, pulls a small biscuit out of the Dutch oven, and hands it to me.

I smile and blow on the biscuit to get it to cool enough for me to eat.

"Mama's biscuits was good, but these are good too. Thank you, Mister Abraham."

I take a big bite from the biscuit and swallow it down slowly, enjoying every bit of the good taste.

"Anyway, Mama went inside the store alone. Said she could think better by herself. We stayed in the wagon with Daddy." I look over at Abraham, sipping loudly on his coffee, chowing down on a biscuit. I can't tell by the look on his face if he believes my story or not, but it don't much matter. I know it's true, every word of it. That all happened back before Daddy showed me lying was okay.

"I need my mama, Mister Abraham. I mean, I'm nearly grown, but that don't mean I don't want my mama close. You know what I mean?" I say, turning from Abraham and swallowing down the lump that's come up in my throat.

"Yes'm. I sho' do know it, missy. I sho' do."

The door to the wagon slings wide and the triplets stumble down the stairs one at a time.

"I'm hungry!" Mac shouts.

"Me too!" Hazel and Filbert say in unison.

Abraham passes out biscuits and I realize that's the end of my storytelling. At least for now.

"We doing a show here?" Filbert asks, chewing the biscuit with his mouth open.

"Don't talk with your mouth full!"

"Aw, Chestnut, you ain't our mama," Mac says, his mouth nearly as fully stuffed as Filbert's. "Stop telling us what to do!"

I shake my head but don't respond. It won't do no good anyhow. I know I'm not their mama but I reckon I'm the closest thing they got to a mama right now. Until I get back to her and put this family back together proper, that is.

Suddenly, Daddy runs into camp like he's being chased by a hungry bear or a mountain lion, his shirttail's hung out and flapping in the breeze, his shoes are untied, and his hair's in a heap of mess. He stops at the edge of the wagon and plops to the ground, looking like something's scared the life plumb out of him. His face is red from the running and the undersleeves of his shirt are as wet with sweat as if he'd taken an afternoon dip in the creek with his clothes on.

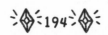

"What's wrong, Slim?" Abraham jumps to his feet. "You a'right? You looks like you done seen a corpse."

Daddy shakes his head, plants his elbows on his knees, and sucks in air harder than anyone I've ever seen. "Abraham . . . take . . . care . . . of . . ."

Before Daddy can finish whatever it is he's trying to say, two men run up behind and snatch him.

"Gotcha!"

My heart sinks, and I feel the fear—gnawing, tearing, pulling fear—down deep inside of me.

28

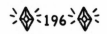

THE BLAME GAME

These are lawmen, it's easy to see, and they lay hands to my daddy in a flash. They're not being gentle about it either. Matter of fact, they jerk him off the ground and sling him around like a vulture picking dry bones in the middle of a dirt-packed road.

"You've got the wrong man! I tell you, I didn't do it!" Daddy hollers, huffing and puffing from the run.

But it's clear to see from the way they're yanking around on him, the men don't believe a word Daddy is saying.

"We know your kind. You've been stealing! The sheriff over in Beaumont says so."

I study the lawman up and down. The name on his tag says Johnny. He's bigger around than he is tall, with hair the color of fresh baked bread and eyes like muddy water. And the smell of him stings my nose. It's strong—like maybe he could use a good long bath.

Mama always says the least anybody can be is clean. Reckon he's never heard tell of soap and water.

"I'm innocent, I tell you!" Daddy yells. "Innocent! I've never stolen anything in my life."

The man slings Daddy around by the arm. As wide-eyed and scared-looking as I've ever seen them, the triplets' mouths are hung to their chests. Hazel's chin is quivering worse than a maple leaf in a windstorm and Mac's chewing his nails like a squirrel would gnaw at a nut.

"What's happening, Chestnut?" Filbert asks, his fists balled like he's ready to jump in and defend Daddy from the trouble.

"Get on up into the wagon," I say as Daddy shoots me a quick look.

They don't move.

"Go on now, I mean it," I say again, taking Hazel by the hand and leading her toward the steps. The boys follow and reluctantly climb the steps and go inside. They stay close to the door though, watching us.

"That's not the way we hear it. The store owner says you left town right after the money went missing. It had to be you. There were no other strangers in town."

"Then again," the lawman says, looking over at Abraham through tiny eye slits, "maybe, it was the Negro that done it. Maybe he's the one stole that money and we've been looking at the wrong man all along."

"No!" Daddy and me shout it at the same time.

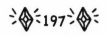

"You leave him alone. He hasn't done anything," Daddy yells. He hangs his head, stares at the ground, and shuffles his foot through the dirt. "I did it. It was me."

He leans over and stares into Johnny's face. "Now you leave him alone, you hear? He's innocent. I'm your man, just like you said." Daddy hangs his head again. "I admit it," he says softly.

"Maybe we ought to run the Negro in too, just in case," the other lawman says. "Maybe they was in cahoots; you know, one playing lookout while the other one stole the money?"

"Say, I never thought about it like that, Will," Johnny says. "You might just have something there."

"You listen here!" Daddy says, through clenched teeth. "Abraham is innocent. He didn't have nothing to do with what I did." Daddy's loud, his words forceful now. "He's innocent, you hear? Leave him alone!"

I swallow hard knowing I'm the only one among the lot of us who knows the truth. I can't believe my daddy, admitting to something he didn't do just to protect a friend.

There's more hullabaloo in the camp than there's ever been. Up in the back of the wagon, the triplets' chins are hung to their chests, eyes bugged out, and it's clear to see they got way more questions than answers.

I look from Daddy to Abraham and back again. Daddy's calm now, like he took a breath, and's not looking for a fight. He looks Sheriff Johnny in the eyes.

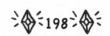

"How did you catch up with me anyway? I mean, how did you know where we were going? I thought we'd outrun you when we left Houston."

"What do you mean outrun us?" Johnny laughs. "You told us exactly where you were headed."

"What?" Daddy eyes Johnny like he's from another world.

"Yep! Easiest thing we've done in a long time was tracking you down! Matter of fact, we didn't have to track you at all. We knew right where you were headed. Couldn't have had a better map if we'd asked for one!" The lawman shoves a wrinkled paper up under Daddy's nose and laughs.

I gasp, realizing it's my words there at the bottom of the paper plain as day.

Heading Next to Dallas, Texas!

There's no use denying it's one of my flyers, complete with striped wagon, Old Stump's backside, yellow wheels and all. Daddy's seen that before, back before it had any words.

He cocks his head and looks at me like I shot him clean through the heart.

My stomach flips and jumps and all I want to do is throw up. It's my own words that's done us in.

"Daddy, I—"

Daddy shakes his head. This time it's him that's not looking me in the eyes.

"It's all right, baby." He shoots me a half-cocked smile. "I don't understand, but it's going to be all right."

For a change I look into his eyes; not only is there fear there, but there's a look of confusion.

Confusion in me.

And what's more, he don't yet know the half of it.

"Stay with Abraham and look after the babies," Daddy says. "We'll get this cleared up just as soon as the officers hear my story."

But I know better. Daddy's going to jail on account of me and can't no amount of his fancy talking clear that up.

The men, one on each side of Daddy, walk him off toward the city and put him into a waiting Model T with a painted star on the side. We watch, none of us saying a word, until the car is clean out of sight.

I want to cry, or scream, or run, but I can't. I look over at Abraham, then back at the triplets.

"Mister Abraham, what's happening?" Mac asks, his chin quivering, and eyes full of baseball tears.

Hazel flings herself to the ground and sobs. Weeping, wailing, hollering sobs. Sounds more like a funeral wake than a sorry-my-daddy's-gone sort of cry.

I run and scoop her up, like I would if I was a shovel and she was a pile of coal. She throws her arms around my neck so hard and fast it chokes me. I cough, and she pulls away, but when she sees I'm all right, she grips me even tighter and sobs like Daddy was killed and not just hauled away.

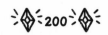

"Aw, Hazel, there ain't no use of all that. He'll be all right," Filbert says. But he's scared too, I can see it in his eyes.

Hazel pulls away, her eyes wide and wild. "Are they gonna . . . gonna hang him?" she asks.

"No, baby, they're not going to hang him."

"Probably lock him up for the rest of his life though," Mac says. "We won't never see our poor old daddy again! He'll be busting rocks on the side of the road with the chain gang."

Hazel lets out another sob. Comes close to busting the drums clean out of my ears.

"Hazel, now stop it! Daddy will get it straightened out," I say, even though I know better. "And you, Mac, you're not helping," I say, shooting a harsh look toward Mac.

I hug Hazel tight, but the hug's as much for me as it is for her. Mama says in times of trouble, what a body needs most is a hug. Daddy's going to jail for something I done, now how do you think that makes me feel?

Awful, that's how I feel, and worse, I know there's no way for him to work it out. He's confessed to a crime he didn't do and the confessing was on account of Abraham—to save his hide from the law.

"Now, now," Abraham says, smiling, but for the first time I don't feel comforted. "Yo' daddy gon' be all right. No need fo' all dat."

"But it ain't right, Mister Abraham! It just ain't right . . ." I say, burying my head in Hazel's hair, pulling her close.

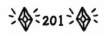

"I tells you what, missy, you stay here with de childrens." Abraham smoothes his hair with his hands. "I'm goin' to walk into town. We needs to know what be's happenin'." He gives me a nod. "I be back afore long."

29

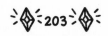

THE SHERIFF

Wait!" I holler, as Abraham walks off. "Do you think you should? I mean, them men was ready to blame you for something you didn't do, all on account of—" I catch myself. No way I would want to hurt Abraham with my words.

"I know, missy," he says, "on accounts of my skin. Now don't you fret 'cause I had dat prob'em all my life and it ain't stop me yet. Man can't help de color o' his skin. Dat's God's doin', and I reckon right now He got work He mean for me to do."

"Yes, but if you go into town and they arrest you too, what'll happen to us?" I point to the triplets. "What'll happen to them?"

Abraham scratches his head. "You might gots somedin' dere, missy."

He looks me up and down, and in my mind I reckon he's studying on whether or not I'm grown up enough to handle this problem.

"Let me go. I can do it, Mister Abraham, really I can. I'll go into town and see what's happening. After all, I'm Daddy's next of kin. They'll have to tell me something."

He scratches his head and rubs his chin, his snowy whiskers making a scratching sound against the skin of his fingers. "Well now, I s'pose dat do makes sense, don't it?" He turns and looks toward town. "You sho' nuff do makes sense."

"I'm sure I ought to go instead."

He looks back at me and nods. "Maybe so," he says.

My stomach is flip-floppin' like a monkey on an elephant ride. I look at the triplets. Hazel's still in a tizzy, sniffing and snubbing around, and Mac's sitting on a log chewing his fingernails into nubs. Filbert's standing, looking toward town, and they's tears streaming down his face.

"All righty den," Abraham says. "You go. But be kerful now, you hear what ol' Abraham say? Be kerful!"

I nod. "Yes, sir, I will."

I take off running as fast as my bony legs will carry me. I've never seen so many high up-in-the-sky buildings in my life, but now ain't the time for looking.

Now's the time for doing.

"Whoa! Whoa! Whoa! There, there, little lady. Where you headed in such a hurry?" A man grabs hold to my shoulders and bends over to look me in the eyes.

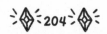

He's a cowboy. I figure that out right away, on account of the hat two times larger than his head, and the boots up to his knees with spurs—shiny, sparkly, pointed spurs on the back of his heels.

"Please, sir, don't hold me," I say. "I got business with the sheriff."

He pushes his large hat to the back of his head with his finger. "With the sheriff? Now what's a pretty little lady like you need with the sheriff?"

"I—need—to—" With every word I jerk, trying to free his hold, but this cowboy's got a grip on me and he's not letting go. I figure there's nothing else I can do, so I don't think twice. I draw back and kick him hard as I can, smacking the middle of his knee, right above the top of his boot.

"Ow!" he bellows, and he lets loose his grip on my shoulders.

I run as fast as I can away from that cowboy, without looking back. Once I realize he's not following me, I slow and glance at the signs on the buildings around me: a bank, a motel, and a restaurant. I breathe deep. The air smells like meat and bread and potatoes, and I can feel my stomach churning. But there's no time for stopping and smelling.

Finally, I reach a brick building with a large sign out front:

SHERIFF'S OFFICE

COUNTY JAIL

Them's the largest doors I ever seen on a building, and folks are coming and going like ants to a picnic. As the doors swing open, a lawman saunters out, and I run in.

The building is humongous with a ceiling that must reach halfway to the sky, the sunshine pushing its way through the windows to light up the inside. From the looks of things at first glance, the building's divided up into sections, just like the inside of an orange. And there's more people milling around wearing fancy lawman uniforms than I ever did see in one place in my life.

"Excuse me, sir? Do you know where I can find the sheriff?" I say to the first man in a suit.

He looks down and gives me a nod. He points off to the side. "Go down that hall to the first door on your left. Can't miss it," he says.

The hall is as long a hall as I've ever seen, but the first door on the left I come to, I go in.

They's chairs, lots of chairs, and books. Stacks and stacks of books. Some of them line the walls, and some of them are propped up on desks; must be twenty or twenty-five desks in this one room alone.

"How may I help you?" the lady behind the longest desk asks. First lady I've seen since I come through the doors. She leans way over the tall desk, I reckon trying to get a better look at the likes of me.

"I come to see the sheriff," I say, right sure of myself, not aiming to let Abraham or my daddy down.

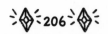

"Now, what's a young'un like yourself needing with the sheriff? Someone stole your candy? Your dog? Your bicycle, perhaps?"

Right off I can see she's a snippy sort, and as she asks what it was that got stole, she pooches out her bottom lip. Now I might be just backwoods country folk, but even the likes of me can see she's poking fun.

"No'm," I say, trying the best I can to be polite, but hoping some way I can change her mind and get her to help me. "I'm here to see to my daddy. Men by the names of Johnny and Will took him away a while ago."

She raises her eyebrows. "Oh, you're *his* daughter? The man they arrested for stealing?"

"Yes, ma'am. I mean, no'm. I mean, I'm his daughter all right, but he didn't do what they said he did."

She turns from me. "Paul, tell Sheriff Nix to come and speak with this young lady, please." She turns back to me. "Just have a seat. He'll be right out."

I never do see "Paul," and I'm sure not about to take a seat like she said. I stand tight where I am and wait.

Seems like hours before the sheriff comes and leans over the table. "You Slim Hill's daughter?" he asks, stretching his neck, looking down on me.

His eyes are large and bulging, like a praying mantis's, and the sides of his bumpy nose spills onto his puffy red cheeks. There's a tiny string of brown spit—tobacco juice I reckon—oozing from one corner of his mouth.

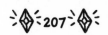

"Yes, sir," I say, suddenly not feeling as brave as before. "I came to see about my daddy."

"We're going to take good care of your daddy. You run along now," he says, thinking he can shoo me away with a wave of his hand.

"Can I see him?"

"Not today."

"But, my daddy's innocent. He didn't steal nothing, honest."

The sheriff and the lady behind the counter look at each other, then back at me.

"Well now, I suppose your daddy's as innocent as all the other daddies we have in here."

The lady laughs and the sheriff smiles.

"Best thing you can do, little lady, is run along back to where you came from. Your daddy will have a trial, same as the others we've got here, and depending on the outcome, he can either go home, or he'll be sent to the penitentiary."

The penitentiary? He didn't steal that money, but if I tell who did, I'll be the one going to the penitentiary and not Daddy. I swallow hard.

"But—"

He interrupts. "We'll be locating your mama and she can come get you and your brothers and sister. Best thing you can do for your daddy now is run along. Jail's no place for a little girl."

I gasp. At long last—my mama! Then in an instant my mind races back to all that's happened and all I've done. I

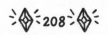

want to see my mama, sure I do. It's what I've dreamed about for two long years, but when she finds out what's really happened—how I've stole and I've lied and how I've got Daddy in more trouble than I could have ever dreamed—why it would just break my poor little mama's heart.

Why just the thought of it all makes my face feel like it's in flames and my hands are as wet with sweat as I can ever remember them being.

I turn to go, but before I do I stop and look back. "But—"

"We'll take care of your daddy; you go on home now," he says.

My heart's in my throat. The man said they was notifying Mama. I should be happy. Instead I'm a-fierce sick. My legs feel like two limp, worn-out rags. Walking out through those doors of the jailhouse, my chin starts to quiver, and I feel the tears rush to the corner of my eyes.

I swipe at my face with the back of my hands and tell myself not to cry, that Mama's coming and everything's going to be all right. But it's not. It's not going to be right and I know it.

Walking back to the campsite, I wonder how a girl like me can have so many mixed up thoughts inside. How did my life go so wrong, so fast? I'm only twelve. All I wanted was to get back to Mama and put our family back together. Is it too much to ask that a girl like me have a happy home?

For the first time since they've been born I dread seeing the triplets, and Abraham too, knowing that there'll be way more

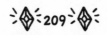

209

questions than I've got answers for. Questions that require a heap more thinking than I've been able to do. Questions that even Mama's coming here can't straighten out.

30

LAWMAN WITHOUT A STAR

The triplets see me coming and run to meet me.

"Where is he?" Mac asks, grabbing my hand and peeping around me like he's expecting Daddy to jump out from behind.

"Is he all right?" Hazel grabs my other hand.

"When's he coming back?" Filbert asks.

"All rights now," Abraham says, "let de girl speak. She gonna tell it all, jes' let de girl speak."

I shake my head and plop down on the ground beside the fire.

"Them biscuits is burned," I say, pointing to the Dutch oven, still buried in the remains of the fire. "I smell them from here."

"Chestnut, don't talk about biscuits," says Filbert. "Talk about Daddy. We want to hear about Daddy."

I shake my head. "They wouldn't let me see him. Said he was in processing or something like that. Sheriff's not a nice man either."

"Did you tell dem yo' daddy an innocent man?" Abraham asks, dipping a cup of water from the bucket and handing it to me.

"I did, Mister Abraham, but they wouldn't believe me. Sheriff said it was for the court to decide."

"What does that mean?"

"It means, Filbert, that Daddy has to have a trial to find out if he did what they say he did. Now the three of you go wash your nasty hands and faces in them water buckets over there."

"But we know he ain't guilty now! We don't need no trial."

"That's the law, Filbert, now wash up. Please." I bury my head in my hands with my elbows propped on my knees feeling like the whole world is sitting on my shoulders.

"Yo' daddy be back soon, missy. He an innocent man. De courts ain't gonna send him down de river 'cause he ain't done it."

"Oh, Mister Abraham," I say with my head still buried in my hands, "this whole thing is way out of control and I don't know how to stop it."

"What you mean, 'dis whole thing'?"

I shake my head.

I can't tell him.

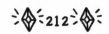

No way he'll understand.

"Ches'nut? What you mean?"

"I can't! I can't, Mister Abraham. I can't tell you. You wouldn't understand."

"Yes I would. You can tell ol' Abraham!"

I take a deep breath. Maybe, just maybe, if he knew, he could—

"Chestnut? Chestnut Hill?"

Lifting my head and giving my face an angry swipe with my hands, I stare through teary eyes. They've come in a car, because they've parked it near Old Stump, but I reckon I was too deep in my thoughts to even notice.

By the solemnness on their faces it's clear. Whoever they are, they've come for me.

"Yes?" I answer reluctantly.

"My name's Norville Bryson, and this is Anita Silverstone."

Another lawman, but without a star, and this time he's brought a woman along. Reckon that's how they do when they come to take a girl to jail—bring a woman with them. I look past him at the lawman's car he got out of.

I stand and clear my throat, giving my face another swipe with my hands. I don't want them thinking I'm weak. "Pleased to make your acquaintance," I say, sticking my hand toward the lady. No way I want them thinking I'm some backwoods bumpkin without manners either, least not while Daddy's locked up behind bars, and not while I don't know if they're aiming to take me in with them. Now's the time for being on my best behavior. Anyway, Mama says manners make the man.

"Likewise, I'm sure," the lady says. She gives a sly sort of look to the lawman like she's surprised I'm not the country hick she thought I'd be.

Right off I notice she's pretty, with a pleasant smile. She's dressed in store-bought fancy clothes, but I don't trust her.

Norville looks at Abraham. "You must be the one they call Abraham," he says.

"Yes, sir." Abraham stretches out his hand to the lawman, then pulls it back slowly.

"Don't worry," Norville says, "I'm not here for you." He snickers.

I look at Abraham, but he's not smiling.

"We're here to take the children."

31

THE END OF A FAMILY

I look to Abraham, feeling a sudden rush of heat come over me. "I . . . I . . . I don't understand."

"It's all right," Anita Silverstone says. "It's for your own good. We're here to take you and your sister and brothers to a foster home."

Mac, Hazel, and Filbert are huddled together at the back of the wagon. If I was to holler "boo" right now, it'd scare the lot of them so bad they'd probably take off running and be clear back to Kentucky before they stopped.

Part of me's relieved that they've not come to lock me up for the stealing I done, but the other part of me is scared, really scared, like a rabbit staring into the eyes of a starving mountain lion sort of scared.

"But, we don't want to go. We're fine here with Mister Abraham," I say.

"Dat's right," Abraham says. "Ol' Abraham ken look after 'em jes' fine."

"Yes, but Abraham is not your guardian," she says, fixing her eyes on me. "He may be your friend, but legally, he can't care for you in your father's absence."

Abraham hangs his head.

"But, I . . . we . . . *no!* We're not going! Our daddy said for us to stay with Mister Abraham and that's what we're aiming to do! You folks can just git! Go on now, git! We're not going," I say, crossing my arms across my chest and locking my knees, suddenly feeling as feisty as my mama.

They look at each other, then back at me.

I hang my head, knowing it's not right, me speaking to the lawman and the lady like I did, but I'm hoping, just this once, it'll be okay. After all, I can't let them take us without a fight. It just wouldn't be proper. Everyone knows young'uns got to fight against being taken away from home against their will.

The triplets, still behind the wagon, are shuffling their feet and whispering.

Anita Silverstone and Norville Bryson don't make a move to go. Fact is, I could practically see their heels digging into the ground.

"Chestnut, this is only temporary," Anita Silverstone says. She moves closer to me and tries to put her hand on my shoulder.

I jerk away.

She clears her throat and takes a step backwards.

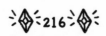

"Sheriff Nix is doing all he can to find your mother. When she comes, you'll be released into her care. In other words, you can leave the foster system. But for now, this is the only way."

I look over at the triplets, as scared as I've ever seen the three of them. Way I figure, it's best to show the babies I'm not afraid and that everything's going to be all right. Sometimes the hardest thing a sister can be is the oldest.

"We want to stay together. We have to stay together—in the same place."

"I'm afraid that's not possible, Chestnut. We have a home that will take the triplets, but four is just too many. There's a nice home for you though, you'll see."

The triplets' heads are hung halfway to their chests. Hazel's chin starts to quiver so I look at her and shake my head "no-no."

They're huddled, looking like they're so confused they don't know their names. Looking at me like they're expecting me to save them from being hauled away.

"Can we get our stuff out of the wagon?" I ask.

Anita Silverstone nods. "Absolutely. Take all the time you need."

"Come on," I say to the triplets, motioning them to follow.

They're about to turn on the waterworks, and truth be told, so am I.

But I can't.

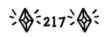

No way I'm going to let any of them see me weak and sniveling. These three babies are looking to me for strength and I'm not about to let them down. I get down on my knees in front of them and look them in the eyes. "Now listen," I say, just as soft as I know how. "This will all be over faster than a cow's tail can flick at a fly. Just do as the lady says and everything will be fine. Anyway, the sheriff's looking for Mama. Isn't that good?" I try to sound encouraging but even I don't believe the words falling from my mouth. I smile, nearly choking on the tears I'm swallowing down.

I nod and do my best to look excited, but I can't.

I want Mama to come. It's everything I been working for, for the longest, but not now. Not like this. Not with Daddy accused of something he didn't do. Somehow, I've got to clear Daddy's name and make this right. But right now, I'm not rightly sure how—without landing behind bars myself, that is.

"Grab up your other set of clothes," I say, "and be quick about it. Let's not keep the folks waiting any longer than need be."

I reach back under my cot, laying hold to my metal box.

"But I want to stay with you," Hazel whines, pulling at my arm.

"Me too," says Filbert, crossing his arms across his chest. "I ain't going. She can't make me."

"Oh, yes she can," I say, "and you are going. So am I. We don't want to give Daddy no cause to worry about us right

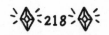

218

now. He's got enough trouble on his plate. We've got to keep a stiff upper lip and just do like we're told. You'll see, this will all be over soon."

I herd the triplets out the door and down the steps. They're clinging to their extra sets of clothes like it's everything they have left in the world.

"All right then," Anita Silverstone says. "Let's all get into the sheriff's car and we'll be on our way."

Filbert and Mac climb in first, without hesitation.

As Hazel starts to climb in, she turns and looks back at the camp. "But what about Mister Abraham? What's gonna happen to him?"

Abraham smiles. "I be's all right, little missy. Don't you worry 'bout ol' Abraham! I's gonna stay wit de wagon 'til yor daddy git back, keep it safe 'til we git back to singin' again. Somebody gots to look after Ol' Stump."

Hazel's chin trembles, and I've got the good sense to know if I don't get her in the car, she's going to be weeping and wailing all over again.

"Come on, Hazel. Mister Abraham will be all right. He'll wait for us and we'll all be back together again soon."

"But you gots lots of money, Chestnut. You can give it to them and they can give it to Daddy, to get him out of jail."

I slap my hand over her mouth and push her into the back of the car.

"What did she say?" asks Anita Silverstone. "What did she mean, 'you've got lots of money'?"

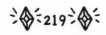

"Oh, it's just my change," I say. "You know, loose change I find on the street? Well, I save it. She gets mixed up sometimes and thinks just because it's change, it's a lot of money." My voice quivers.

I climb in the car and give Hazel an if-you-open-your-mouth-again-I'll-kill-you look.

As the car drives away, I blink over and over again, trying my best to keep the tears from falling. I don't dare look out the window at Abraham or Old Stump or the wagon.

"Let me take that box and put it up front for you," Norville Bryson says, reaching over the seat for my box.

I clutch it to my chest. "No, thank you," I say, shooting him the same look I gave Hazel.

He draws his hand back fast, like I'd slapped it. Reckon with my eyes, I did.

We ride for a while, first through the middle of town with buildings packed together tight, and then into areas with hills that roll, dotted with houses like the hide on a white-tailed fawn.

I don't say it out loud but I can't help but think this is the end of our family. Mama is who knows where; I'm not even sure the sheriff will be able to find her. Daddy's in jail, and the triplets and me is going to be split up. I might never see any of them again. And to top it all off, now I've got to worry about Hazel spilling the beans about the money she's seen.

I swallow hard and stare mindlessly out the window. I wanted so much to put this family back together. I've lied—

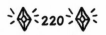

just the way Daddy taught me—so that he could sell elixir and make money to get Mama a nice house, but Daddy never was meaning to get back to Kentucky. That was clear from every word that come out of his mouth. It just took me longer to figure it out than it should have. Maybe now I see that going home was all just a dream that was never gonna happen in the first place. I thought if I could just get to Mama she'd make everything right. Now I've made it so's our whole family might never be together again.

I've looked after the triplets best any sister could. Took food out of my mouth so's they could eat, kept them clean and out of harm's way, and tried to teach them important things, like how to spit and the proper way to make an acquaintance.

I've stole money so I could buy a train ticket, get back to Mama, and put our family back together. I drew up flyers so that if Mama came searching, she could find us, but instead it led the lawmen right to our camp. Now my daddy's in jail and may be going to prison for a long, long time on account of something I done.

I've messed up, but I only wanted to put things back together. Right now I can't stand myself, and it would serve me right to be the one in jail instead of Daddy.

Another time I'd be excited to get my first car ride. Today, it seems to be making me sick.

After a while, Norville Bryson stops the car in front of a large brick home. There are rocking chairs on the front porch, flower baskets hanging low, and a big yellow dog stretched out in the sun in the yard. There's a lady and a man standing arm in arm on the porch, smiling and waving at the car like we're their long-lost relatives coming for a visit.

Anita Silverstone gets out of the car first. She walks around and opens the door on the other side from where I'm sitting.

"Macadamia, Filbert, Hazelnut," she says, "this is where you'll be staying."

She leans in and looks at me. "Chestnut, you sit tight. I'll be back soon as I get the triplets situated." She smiles a goofy sort of smile.

The triplets each give a last teary look as they tumble from the car.

"Chestnut?" Hazel questions, her cheeks flushed and a strange sort of puzzled look on her face. "Do we have to?"

I nod and flash her a fake smile. I'd like to offer up some comforting words but know that if I speak, angry words, hurtful words might come pouring out of my mouth. And hurtful words are not the words I want the triplets to remember from their big sister—especially if it's the last time we'll be together.

"But, when will we see you again?" Mac asks, his hands trembling by his side.

I give Filbert a look and he nods and swipes at his eyes with the back of his wrist. He drapes his arm around Mac and they slowly turn to go.

They inch the walkway together, like three children on their way to face the gallows.

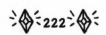

The lady and man, arm in arm on the porch, come down the walkway to greet the triplets. They hug them and smile like they was all long-lost friends.

Norville Bryson, looking toward the walkway, grunts. He gives a short look to me in the back seat, then turns and stares straight ahead.

I may never see them again, but I don't cry. Reckon a body would have to feel something in order to be able to cry. Right now all I feel is . . . numb.

32

No One to Greet Me

Anita Silverstone gets back into the car and sighs, like she's relieved she done her job.

"Now, that wasn't so bad, was it?" she asks, leaning over the front seat, looking square at me.

Oh, she's proud of what she done—that's easy to see. Maybe taking three young'uns away from their big sister isn't so bad to her, and maybe knowing she's splitting up a family forever might not be so awful to her way of thinking, but the way I see it, it's worse than taking a licking any day of the week.

Reckon it's a good thing poor Mama isn't here to see what's happening to her babies. Her heart would break into so many pieces there's nothing yet been invented that could put it all back together again.

My heart's breaking too, in smeared shades of pencil lead, burnt wood, and storm clouds, running like salty tears on a bumpy, scratched-up canvas.

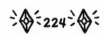

Anita Silverstone turns and faces the front of the car, and it's just as well. I've got nothing to say to a woman that's got no more regard for family than to split up young'uns like she done.

We ride for a while, and at first I try to remember every turn in every bend of the road, so's I can get back to the triplets if I need to. But after a while we take so many twists and turns, past so many low-lying buildings and hills with barns and hills without barns, I couldn't find my way back if I wanted to.

Norville Bryson pulls the car up to a house smaller than the one for the triplets. With its smoky gray outside walls and black shutters that could stand to have another coat of paint slathered on them, it suits my mood to a tee.

There are no rockers on the porch and no flower baskets hanging low. The grass is ankle high to a giraffe and the yard looks like it's not been took care of in more weeks than I can count.

No one's here to greet me. No one smiling and waving. No one's on the walk, to go with me inside. All I see is one lone pumpkin-orange cat with a long striped tail, curled up in front of the door.

I stay sitting in the car until Anita Silverstone opens my door. "Ready?" she asks, smiling a silly-looking smile like she's expecting me to jump out, kiss her hand, and thank her for taking away my family and making it so's we'll never again be together.

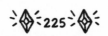

I shoot her one last look before getting out of the car.

I want to tell her I think she's sly, and dirty, and can't be trusted. I want to tell her I hate her for coming to our camp with that Norville Bryson lawman and snatching us away from everything we've known. I want to scream that I think she's going to the devil for taking us away from Mister Abraham, and from Old Stump, and from the wagon—our home. But I can't.

I can't because I know she's not the reason for all this. Norville Bryson the lawman's not either. It's not Daddy, or Abraham, or Sheriff Nix, or even the store owner back in Beaumont.

It's me.

It's all on account of me.

I'm the reason my family's destroyed, and I deserve every bad thing that comes to me.

"You're really going to like it here," Anita Silverstone says. "The lady's elderly, but she's kind, and she's looking forward to having a youngster in the house again."

"Did you tell her I'm not staying?" I say, clutching my metal box in one hand, and my change of clothes in the other.

"She knows."

I walk to the porch beside Anita Silverstone. The orange cat yawns and stretches without moving a lick as Anita Silverstone knocks on the wooden screen door.

For the longest time, I don't hear anything.

She knocks again.

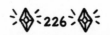

After a while, there's the shuffling of feet along the floor.

"Coming!" a voice hollers from inside.

When the lady gets to the door, I can't believe my eyes.

33

But . . . This Ain't Home

The lady on the other side of the door is more than old. She's ancient.

From the looks of her she must be nigh on a hundred with hair the color of goat's milk and eyes like the sky—covered with splotchy gray clouds. She's stooped and bent at the waist and her hands are knobby and twisted. In one hand she's toting a long walking stick, with the other, she grips to the doorframe.

She starts to push open the screen door, then holds it until Anita Silverstone catches it and pulls it open the rest of the way.

"Chestnut, this is Mrs. Wallace. Mrs. Wallace, this is Chestnut Hill."

I stretch my hand toward her and she places hers in mine. It's gnarled and veiny, and her grip is all but absent, but I curl my fingers around it and give a gentle shake, up and down.

"Pleased to make your acquaintance, ma'am. Thank you for letting me stay awhile with you."

"Well now," Mrs. Wallace says, smiling sweetly and glancing at Anita Silverstone, "we're going to get on just fine."

She looks me up and down, smiling again when she looks into my eyes. Her voice is weak and shakes like fresh jelly when she talks; her words are deliberate and slow.

"You'll have the entire upstairs to yourself," she says. "I've long since given up climbing stairs. Go on up and just make yourself at home. Arrange things how you'd like."

I look at Anita Silverstone.

She nods and winks.

"Thank you, ma'am. I'll do my best not to cause you any hardship," I say, taking the stairs two by two, hoping to reach the bedroom before she changes her mind. At the top of the stairs I peek over the railing and listen, to see if they'll talk about me now that I'm gone.

"What a delightful young lady," says Mrs. Wallace. "And such manners!" She takes Anita Silverstone by the arm. "Now don't you worry about a thing; we'll be fine. You can check on us any time you like, but I really don't think it will be necessary."

"Thank you, Myrtle," says Anita Silverstone, closing the door behind her.

The upstairs is a spacious loft with a large window at one end draped heavy with white-laced, billowy curtains, pulled to one side. There's a bed large enough for sleeping the triplets

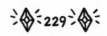

and me against the wall, draped with the prettiest blue and white quilt I ever did see. There's a large chest against one wall with room enough inside for hanging dresses, and a lamp with dangling beads hanging from its edges on top of a small square table by the bed.

I pull down the covers and press my nose into the sheets, breathing in deep. Aah! Sunshine and fresh air, reminding me of wash day back home, with clean clothes slapping the summer breeze, Mama shooing away the crows, and the babies playing in the sunshine under the clothesline.

"Feel free to light the kerosene lamp if you want, dear," Mrs. Wallace yells from downstairs. "When you've settled in, come on down and we'll have a bite to eat."

Running to the top of the stairs I holler back, "Yes, ma'am, I'll be right down."

This room is the prettiest thing I ever laid eyes on and practically perfect for a girl my age—or a girl of any age really. What a nice change to be in a home that don't move, with walls and a ceiling and real stairs that don't wiggle when you climb them. It almost makes me feel as happy inside as Christmas morning back home. But . . . this ain't home . . .

I think back to the wagon where our four cots line the walls and the only light is from the barred windows on the sides. Most of the time there's mud covering the floor from the boys' shoes, and it's hard to keep from tripping over marbles and jacks and coloring books strewn from end to end.

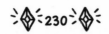

In my head I believe I could stay here forever, but in my heart, I know it's not for long.

I run down the stairs, careful not to step on the pumpkin-colored cat with the long striped tail that's stretched across the length of the bottom step. It stands, slowly stretches, and then rubs against my legs, like it's trying its best to rub away every bit of its fur.

Mrs. Wallace appears in the doorway and smiles.

"Oh, my dear, I do hope you like cats," she says. "Lollipop surely seems to like you, doesn't she?"

"Yes'm," I say, "I like cats just fine, even though I've never been close enough to pet one before."

"You've never stroked a cat?"

"No, ma'am. Back home we mostly had dogs, but they wasn't for stroking, they was for hunting and protecting the house from coyotes and the likes."

"Well, come on into the kitchen now and we'll talk. I want to know all about your home."

Mrs. Wallace tugs the light blue shawl draping her shoulders tighter around her neck. She shuffles toward the kitchen and I walk close behind, taking in everything I see. From the outside, no way anyone would dream what a fine house this is. It's so clean and smells so fresh, and the afternoon sun lends a warm, friendly glow to its middle.

If I believe Daddy's story, this must be what Mama's been wanting—one of these fresh-smelling houses with quilts on the bed and a cat in the parlor. Now I understand that what

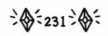

Mama wanted was springtime in April, but all Daddy could give her was the ice of December.

"What are these?"

Mrs. Wallace chuckles. "Those are doilies, dear. They're placed on the chair arms and backs for the purpose of absorbing body oils that might damage the furniture. My things are old, but I do my best to keep them clean."

She stops, turns, and looks up into my eyes.

"Don't you be afraid of soiling things though. I want you to feel comfortable and at home as much as you can under the circumstances."

Her words are reassuring but they set my mind to racing. What does she know about my circumstances? What did Anita Silverstone tell her?

"Come. Sit. Let's eat, my dear."

The kitchen is small but cozy, and smells of fresh baked bread. The table's set fancy enough for a queen, with plates of blue and white. She calls them her "Blue Willows."

When she's not looking I run my fingers along their edges. Humph. No cracks or chips.

She serves sandwiches of pimento cheese, beside a steaming hot bowl of tomato soup. And there's potato chips too, that still have the crunch. She's poured tall glasses of orange juice—fresh too many days ago to count—that now tastes of a tang. I don't say anything about it though. No need to hurt her feelings, especially when I can see how hard she's trying to make things right.

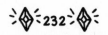

We sit for a while and eat, but we don't talk. New to each other like we are, I reckon neither of us can think of anything to say, but the silence is comfortable and friendly.

"I hope you will be comfortable here, dear, and you're welcome to stay as long as you need. It sounds as though you've been through quite an ordeal. I'm sorry for that," she says after a bit.

I wait for her to say more, but she don't and now I know that Anita Silverstone must have spilled the beans. I take a bite of sandwich and wash it down with a spoonful of soup.

"My daddy didn't do what they say."

She don't look up from spooning her soup. She don't say a word.

"My mama will be here soon, and we're going to be a family again."

I glance at her, expecting a raise of her eyebrows or even just a questioning look, but it don't come. And still, she doesn't say a word. I'm not sure if she don't hear me or if she's just not quite in the mood to speak—after all, I've not been around old folk much, at least not for long at a time.

"Do you know I have two brothers and a sister?" I speak louder this time, so's there's no doubt she can hear me.

"Oh yes, dear," she says. "I know all about you." She raises her eyebrows and smiles.

I knew it! Anita Silverstone can't be trusted. Blabbermouth.

No more words are said between us at that meal, but it's all right with me. Lends more time for eating, and eat I do. Lickety-split. I'd lick my bowl if I could, but it wouldn't be proper. No use Mrs. Wallace thinking me a backwoods bumpkin this soon after I've come. No, sir. Anyway, if I was to lick my bowl it would only be when she turned her head and wasn't looking. After all she moves so slow . . .

"Thank you for the food," I say, carrying my plate and bowl to the sink.

"You're welcome, dear. Just leave them there and I'll wash them later. You go on up and rest now. It will be getting dark soon." When I reach the stairs I hear her say, "That attic gets a bit warm in the evenings. Feel free to throw back the quilt and open a window if you need. Oh, and if you'd like, I'll put the kettle on and get some water to boiling for you to have a nice bath in the washtub out on the side porch."

Running the stairs two at a time I holler, "Thank you, ma'am," loud enough so's I'm sure she can hear.

Lollipop's curled on the bed, with pillows to her back. I fall onto the bed beside her and stare up at the ceiling. This would be a fine adventure for a girl like me, and a fine room for a girl to grow up in—if that girl didn't have so much on her mind that is. And just like that my mind's back on my daddy.

Here I am, lying on a soft, fresh-smelling bed with warm food in my belly and a fluffy autumn cat curled up and snoring next to me. Daddy don't have none of that. He's in a cold, wet jail cell, with nothing to eat but a slice of bread and a glass of water to drink. And it was me that put him there.

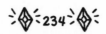

Suddenly, the warm soup and sandwich don't sit so well in the bottom of my belly, and I have to swallow to keep it down.

I think about Abraham, and how he keeps saying Daddy is a good man; that Daddy gives away his money to orphans and widow women and how it takes a mighty big man to give to others when he could keep the money himself and get rich if he'd want.

I turn and face the wall, knowing I have the power to change it. But, if I do, it'll be me in that jail cell with only bread and water. There won't be none of these fine things anymore, and I won't ever see the light of day again.

Oh, how I wish Sheriff Nix would find my mama. She'd know just what to do.

I reckon it's then I fall asleep, Daddy's plight—and mine— weighing heavy on my mind and heart.

34

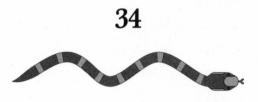

Nothing So Terrible
as a Conscience

Sunshine announces itself the next day through the large
window behind my head, and for just a second my troubles are far removed from my mind.

While I snuggle under the covers, Lollipop purrs and nuz-
zles me like a horse begging for a sugar cube. It puts me in the
mind of Old Stump and, just that quick, my troubles return.
Mama says troubles are only as far away as a memory, and
Mama sure was right.

I wonder how Abraham's getting on.

Feeling under my pillow for my metal box, I open it and
stare at the money inside—the money that caused all this
trouble. It glares at me, lifeless and cold, like a gigantic boul-
der on the side of a creek bank. I slam the box and quick as I
can, shove it back under the pillow.

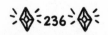

I breathe in deep, smelling smells I've not smelled in forever. Bacon! Not since Kentucky have I smelled bacon!

I jump from the bed and pull up the covers, smoothing the quilt as best I can. I press down my pillow hair and run the stairs to greet Mrs. Wallace.

"Good morning, sunshine," she says. She's already sitting at the table, sipping on coffee and juice.

The table's set with the same blue and white plates and glasses of juice as yesterday. I sip the juice. It has the same tang. 'Bout chokes me to death, but I do my best not to let on.

They's biscuits stacked like the Tower of Babel on a plate in the middle of the table with strawberry jelly, apple butter, and another plate plumb full of long strips of crispy bacon.

I look around the kitchen and then around the corner into the other room.

"Anything wrong, dear?"

"Oh, no, ma'am," I say. "I'm just looking for the others."

"What others?" she asks, sipping her coffee and nibbling on a biscuit.

"The others that are coming to eat with us."

Mrs. Wallace laughs. "No one else is coming, dear."

"Then, who's all this food for?" I ask, shaking my head and rubbing my eyes.

"Why, you and me of course!" Mrs. Wallace says smiling, her eyes so kind and gentle I barely notice the clouds that cover the blue.

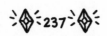

"Wow! I've never seen this much food for just two people in all my life. You mean I can have two biscuits if I want, and jelly, and apple butter, too?" My smile stretches my face.

"Two, three, however many you want, dear, and all the bacon you'd like, too. You eat until you're filled to the brim and can't take in another bite. Then, we'll have lunch!" Mrs. Wallace claps, leans back in her chair, and laughs.

Her laugh is consoling, and for just a few seconds I forget why I'm here. What I been wanting for the last two years is all I can eat of something. Anything. Now that I got it, it's almost more than I can take in. My belly's stretching just thinking about it being full.

But all at once, a terrible sinking feeling overtakes me.

"What's the matter, dear?" Mrs. Wallace asks, suddenly somber and serious. "Are you all right? Why, you're as pale as a sheet."

I look over all the good food Mrs. Wallace has on the table. Seems like all of a sudden, I don't want it any more, that what's important isn't the food, or the belly full, or being able to eat all I want of something.

"What's wrong, dear?" She gently places her knobby hand on top of mine. "Now that I look closer, you do look a bit tired. Didn't you sleep well, dear?"

I nod.

"Don't you like biscuits and bacon? Aren't you fond of jelly?"

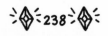

"Oh, yes, ma'am," I say. "I like it fine. Reckon I'm just not as hungry as I thought."

I feel my smile shrinking right along with my belly.

Staring into my lap, I think about what I done and how I ruined everything for everybody, destroying a whole bunch of lives: my daddy's, the triplets', and Abraham's. And what's more I'm the only one can fix things and set them right. I wonder if I've got the courage it takes to do it?

"Mrs. Wallace?"

"Yes, dear?"

"Um . . . well . . ."

"What's bothering you, dear? Something you'd like to talk about? I might not have the answers, but I can do what old women do best, and that's listen."

I want to talk.

I want to tell her what I done.

I want to sling this weight from my shoulders and tell her right out loud how I've lied, and what I've stole, and what a horrible person I really am.

Since Daddy was an orphan and Mama's mama and daddy died before I ever knew them, I never had a grandma or grandpa to ask questions to. Mrs. Wallace might be someone I could think of as a grandmother—if times and things were different, that is. But thinking of her like a grandmother almost makes it worse.

No way I want her thinking bad of me.

No way I want her knowing she's got a thief living and breathing right here in her house.

"No, ma'am. I reckon not. May I be excused, please?"

"But, dear, you haven't eaten a thing."

"I know. Reckon I've lost my appetite."

For three days I can't eat and I can't sleep. I lie on the bed with Lollipop by my side and stare at the ceiling. When darkness overtakes my room, I toss and turn from side to side and wait for morning to come. They's an elephant jumping up and down on my chest and a lump big as a camel's hump plugging my throat. When the sun finally stares in the window and it's time to begin the day, I'm almost sorry. With the feelings of dread in my belly, all I want is for nighttime to come again so I can be alone—under the cover of darkness. Mrs. Wallace says stroking a cat is good for everything that ails you. I'm feared Lollipop's about to lose every bit of her fur.

And I'm feared too that Mrs. Wallace knows why. Oh, she looks at me and smiles that sweet, cloudy-eyed smile, but deep down I think she knows what I done. She knows I'm the reason my daddy's locked up; I'm the reason my family's torn apart.

I know what I need to do. I know what I need to do, but I've not seen hide nor hair of Anita Silverstone, Norville Bryson, or Sheriff Nix. And I've not heard a word about my mama.

Until today.

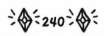

"Chestnut, dear?" Mrs. Wallace calls from the bottom of the stairs. "Would you come down, please? There's someone to see you."

I shove my metal box with the evil stolen money inside up under my pillow. I smooth out the wrinkles of the quilt so no one will know they's something under them pillows, give Lollipop a scruffing, and lean over and kiss her head.

"Coming!" I holler, my mind in a tizzy wondering who could be here to see me. Maybe, just maybe . . .

I can barely breathe thinking about who it might be, and then I look to the door.

"Chestnut?"

It's not who I wanted to see.

But it is, I reckon, who I need to lay eyes to.

35

FULL BELLIES AND BOOKS

Chestnut, would you like to visit your daddy?" Anita Silverstone asks, smiling from ear to ear like now *she's* the one that swallowed down the canary.

I look to Mrs. Wallace, asking permission to go.

"Well by all means, dear, go! Go, and tell your daddy hello! Have a nice long visit. Lollipop and I will be here when you get back."

"Sure," I say to Anita Silverstone. "Can we go and see the triplets too?"

"Why not?"

I follow her outside, waving good-bye to Mrs. Wallace on our way to the car. Norville Bryson, leaning against the car, nods and tips his lawman hat.

"I'll tell you what," says Anita Silverstone. "Why don't we pay a visit to your brothers and sister first? Afterwards, we'll go and see your father. Oh, and, Chestnut, I have another surprise for you."

Wondering what her surprise could be, I look to her like she's my best friend in the whole world. But I don't believe it. How could I trust a woman who divides families for a living and splits up young'uns like bad apples from a basket?

"Sheriff Nix has located your mother. She'll be arriving on the afternoon train."

I can't believe it! My mama! My dear, sweet, loving mama. I've waited more than two years to see her, and today's the day my dream's going to come true.

"You mean it? You really mean it? My mama's coming, today?"

"Yes! I thought you might be excited about that."

All of a sudden they's a million ideas swirling around in my head like acorns in a hurricane. Has she changed? Will she know me when she sees me? Will she think I've grown into a woman now? Will she know the triplets? They've grown so since she's seen them.

And then it hits me. Daddy. She's coming here because Daddy's in jail.

What's Mama going to say? Will she forgive Daddy? Will they fuss or will they kiss and make up?

What about when she finds out what I done? Will I ever get to be with Mama and Daddy and the triplets after I'm arrested and thrown in the pokey for thieving?

This car ride that began so much better than I remember from the last time is turning out to be just as much of a disappointment.

Norville Bryson pulls the car in front of the large brick house with the rocking chairs on the front porch, flower baskets hanging low, and a big yellow dog in the yard. The triplets are there too, playing with the dog. They don't even turn to look at the car. There's more laughing, more squealing, and more hooting than I can remember hearing since we left Kentucky. Even the blindest man in the county could see the triplets are happy where they are.

Anita Silverstone gets out, opens my door, then slams it behind me. Still, the triplets don't look. If I didn't know better, I'd think they'd gone deaf.

"Chestnut!" Filbert yells, as we start down the walk toward the house. "Hey, look everybody, it's Chestnut!"

They run down the walk and grab hold to me, the yellow dog bounding behind. After the greetings, Anita Silverstone and Norville Bryson go inside the large brick house and leave me and the triplets outside to ourselves.

"Hazel, Mac, you and Filbert come to the porch and let's sit a spell and talk," I say, walking toward the porch, expecting them to follow me, expecting to be accosted with stories of what they've been doing and how they've been getting on. But it's like they don't hear a thing.

Now that the excitement's worn off, it seems the yellow dog's got more of a draw with them three than their big sister.

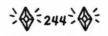

"Filbert, have you read any books you want to tell me about?"

Filbert tosses a ball to Mac, over the head of the dog.

"Mac, don't you want to tell me what you've been doing? Did these people get you a yo-yo? I know you left yours back at the wagon with Mister Abraham."

Mac tosses the ball to the dog.

"Hazel, come talk to me." I motion her over with my hand, but it seems that she's turned every bit of her attention to the dog.

"Filbert, guess where I'm going?"

Filbert don't look my way.

"I'm going to go see Daddy," I holler, but he acts like he don't care.

I jump to my feet and run into the yard, stepping in the middle of their game. I snatch Hazel by the arm.

"Ouch! Chestnut, you're hurting me!" she yells. "Leave me alone. I want to play." She breaks free my hold and runs back to the dog.

"But don't you care that I'm going to go and see Daddy?" I ask. Knowing Hazel like I do, I'm sure when she understands I'm really going to visit Daddy she'll stop playing and pay attention.

"Listen, you three," I say. "I want to talk to you. We haven't seen each other in a long time. Come over here and sit down."

Plopping down on the porch, I pat the step beside me with my hand.

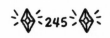

"Chestnut, you ain't our boss," says Hazel.

"I'm not trying to be your boss. I just want to talk. Don't you have something you want me to tell Daddy? Like you love him, or that you can't wait to get back to the wagon, or that you miss him terribly?"

Filbert stops playing with the dog, ambles to the porch, and drops to the steps to sit.

"Filbert, you miss Daddy, don't you?"

"Well sure I do, Chestnut, but . . ."

"But what?"

"Well, it's just that I like it here too. I mean, these folks are nice, and, Chestnut, guess what?" His eyes that remind me so much of the ocean sparkle in the light of the sun. "They let us have all we want to eat!"

"Yeah," hollers Mac, "and they bought us new clothes. They even said we could stay with them forever if we want. They said they got a nice school here with lots of young'uns our age."

"And," says Filbert, "they got a nice teacher and all the books we ever want to read. Books about friends, and horses, and—"

"And pirates!" yells Mac. "Don't forget about the pirates!"

I can't believe what I'm hearing. We've not been separated more than a week and a half and the triplets got a new home. They've done forgot about Daddy, and about Abraham, and the elixir, and—

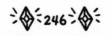

"Hey, Chestnut!" Mac hollers. "You can tell Daddy I love him, but don't tell him nothing else. I mean, don't tell him I got new clothes, or a new house, or a dog or nothing about a new school, all right?"

"Yeah, me too," says Filbert. "I mean, I miss Daddy and all, but well, it's awfully nice here. I mean, it's a nicer place than any place I ever been, and we don't ever have to go to bed with our bellies growling, or dig for food in trash cans, or nothing."

"But we're family. You can't just throw away family, even for food and fancy clothes."

They don't even look at me and I wonder if all the food they've had to eat has clogged up their minds as well as their hearts.

"There's something else I want to tell you," I say, catching Filbert's eyes when I say it. "Mama's coming today."

Mac and Hazel stop their playing and turn to stare at me. Seems my words have stunned all three of them, and Filbert's looking like he doesn't understand a word I just said.

36

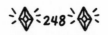

Forgetting Mama

Mama's coming," I say again.

They don't move.

"That woman, Anita Silverstone, told me so. She said Mama's coming on the afternoon train. Don't you want to see Mama?"

Hazel looks at Mac and Mac looks at Filbert. It's like the cat's snatched all three of their tongues clean out of their mouths and can't none of the three of them speak a word.

Filbert stares at the ground and what he says next comes close to worrying the life plumb out of me.

"Chestnut, I don't really remember Mama. I mean, I remember we had a mama but not exactly what she was like."

"You don't remember our loving mama? Filbert, you know you remember Mama."

"I don't remember her neither," Hazel says. "I mean, I remember that her hands were soft and that she laughed a lot, but not what she looks like."

"You do, don't you, Mac? You remember what she looks like, don't you?"

Mac shakes his head then drops to his knees to pet the dog.

My heart's broke into a million tiny slivers. I can't believe them babies don't remember Mama. Two years is a long time, yes, but not so long that you forget your mama for goodness sakes. They was just four, almost five, when Daddy run off with us, but looks to me like they ought to remember something.

"I just don't know who any of you are anymore. You ain't paid me no more attention than a bag of rocks since I come until right this second, and I had to practically beg you for that. You want to forget about Daddy and go to living with folk we don't even know, and now, worst of all, you don't remember your own mama. I can't believe it. I just can't . . ."

Burying my head in my hands, I want to bust out crying, but I can't.

I won't!

No way I'm going to let that Anita Silverstone, or Norville Bryson, or the triplets, or anybody for that matter see me cry!

I. Got. My. Pride!

Filbert jumps to his feet and the triplets go back to playing with the yellow dog, like our conversation never took place. I stare across the yard, and the more I think on it, the more I know without a doubt what I've got to do. I've got to put an end to all this madness and I've got to do it now. No matter what it costs me.

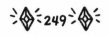

Stomping across the porch I pound on the door.

Anita Silverstone comes to the door in a rush. "Chestnut, is everything all right?"

"Yes, ma'am, but I'd like to go and see my daddy now."

"What? Oh, all right. So, you've visited enough with your brothers and sister?"

She stretches her neck and looks across the yard to the triplets, running and playing with the yellow dog like I haven't even been here and they've not heard one word spewed out of my mouth.

"Yes, ma'am," I say, and I turn and walk back across the lawn to the car.

When we're all in, I look back at the triplets, expecting them to wave and holler good-bye, but they don't. Matter of fact they don't even look my way—again. And my feelings is hurt clear through to the bone.

"Mrs. Silverstone?" I ask, still staring out the window at the triplets. "Could I please go back to Mrs. Wallace's house before I visit my daddy?"

"Now? Before you see him?" she asks, turning in the seat to look at me.

"Yes, ma'am, please. There's something I forgot to get when we left."

"All right," she says, looking at Norville Bryson. "But you won't be able to take anything in with you when you see your daddy, you know."

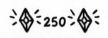

"Yes, ma'am. I understand, but there's something I need. Something I have to have when I go to the jail."

Norville Bryson looks at Anita Silverstone with questions on his face. She shrugs like she doesn't have a clue what I'm talking about.

And she doesn't. No one does. Only me, and the Good Lord Above know what I'm planning.

Norville Bryson turns the car around and drives all the way back to Mrs. Wallace's house.

"Do you want me to come in with you?" Anita Silverstone asks.

"No. I'll be right back."

I run to the door and knock.

And I knock.

And I knock.

The trouble with old people is not their age, it's that they're slow. Slower than sorghum molasses in an ice storm, but, bless her heart, she's the sweetest old lady I ever did meet in my whole entire life.

"Well, hello, dear! Back so soon? I barely knew you were gone," she says, shuffling to the door and cracking the screen just enough for me to take hold and open it the rest of the way.

"Yes, ma'am. I mean, no, ma'am. I mean, I forgot something. I'll just run upstairs and get it and then we'll be on our way again."

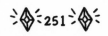

"All right, dear," Mrs. Wallace says. "Take your time."

I jump the steps two at a time.

I run across the room to the bed and pull back the covers, shoving my hand up under the pillows and laying hold to my metal box. The money's still there, every piece of it.

Slamming the lid, I pull the box to my chest and jump down the stairs faster than I went up. Mrs. Wallace is at the bottom, her light blue shawl draped loose around her shoulders, with Lollipop under one arm and her stick in her other.

I pat Lollipop on the head, give a quick scratch behind her ears, and lean over and kiss her between the eyes.

Mrs. Wallace smiles. "Get what you need, dear?"

"Yes, ma'am. Sorry to trouble you. I'll be back soon," I holler, running across the porch and back to the car. But I know better.

I won't be back.

I'll be in jail.

"What do you have there?" Norville Bryson asks, glancing over his shoulder as he drives.

Now, I'm not aiming to be rude and I'm not aiming to be snippy, but the way I see it my box is none of his business. So, trying the best I can not to be ugly, I say, "Just something I need," in as polite a voice as I can muster.

In the mirror I see him raise his eyebrows at Anita Silverstone.

Seems like the sheriff's office and county jail is a long, long ways away from Mrs. Wallace's house, especially in the

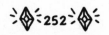

silence of that car. I'm happy though, because the way I've got it figured, I've got to do way too much thinking to be carrying on a conversation right now.

The sheriff's office is just as I remember, but a different lady's behind the desk asking folks to sit and wait their turn.

Anita Silverstone's asking me to wait too. She points to a chair and says, "Take a seat, Chestnut. We'll go to see your father in a moment. I need to take care of a few things first."

I clutch my metal box; after all we're in the sheriff's office. Who knows how many thieves might be lingering around, waiting to steal it.

Anita Silverstone is gone for a long time, longer than I reckoned she would be. Watching folks come and go I wonder what's become of my daddy. After sitting so long my legs go to sleep, I stand, walk over, and catch the eyes of the lady behind the desk.

"Excuse me, ma'am," I say, in as respectful a voice as I know how. "Would it be all right if I talk to the sheriff? Sheriff Nix, I mean."

"What do you need him for?" she asks, without looking up from her papers.

"I need to talk with him about something," I say. "Something that's important to my daddy."

"Sheriff Nix is busy," she says, glaring over the table at me. "Anyway, he doesn't have time for children."

"But, I'm not children, I'm twelve. Anyway, I've got business with him."

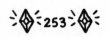

"Now what kind of business could you possibly have with the sheriff, hmm?"

She gives me a look that says she's not got time for the likes of me. I figure then, if I want Sheriff Nix, I'll have to find him myself.

"Paul!" I hear a man holler from another room, "take these papers down to processing, will you?"

"Yes, Mister Nix," I hear a voice say. I still don't see anybody named Paul anywhere. There's no one in the office but me and the lady behind the desk. Anita Silverstone's in another room and Sheriff Nix is in his office, I suppose.

I look at the sign on the wall, the sign next to the two double doors.

OBADIAH NIX
HIGH SHERIFF

Somehow, I've got to get past this lady and into the sheriff's office. I need to talk to him. Alone.

Anita Silverstone comes back into the office carrying a large stack of papers.

"Chestnut, I'm almost finished, and then we'll go in to see your father, all right?"

She plops the stack of papers in front of the lady at the desk and then walks off. The lady behind the desk sighs. She grabs up a handful of the papers and walks, in a hurry, out

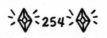

the door and down the hall. I look around the office. There's no one here but me.

I take a deep breath and grit my teeth, reckoning there's no time like right now to do what I've got to do. I pull my box close and step off to the sheriff's office.

37

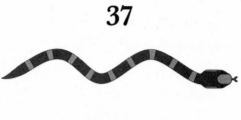

PROOF

I clutch my box tight, shove my nose up toward the ceiling, and walk through the double doors to see the sheriff.

Daddy says if there's something you want to do and you don't have the nerve, keep a stiff upper lip, square back your shoulders, and say what it is you want to say as fast as you can—before you lose your nerve.

That's exactly what I'm aiming to do.

I see the sheriff sitting behind a big black desk, leaning against the wall in the largest chair I ever did see. He's not a big man. What I mean is, I don't think he's a tall man, but laid back in the chair like he is, I'm having to look way up to see into his eyes.

I walk right in—acting as if I own the place—and at first, the sheriff don't look up. But when he does, you'd have thought from the look on his face that I'd pulled a musket from my boots and cocked it.

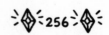

"Who let you in here?" he asks, grabbing to the desk and hanging on for dear life. His eyes are jumping around the room like he's searching for someone to blame for letting a young'un like me into his office without permission.

He leans way over on his desk, crosses his arms, and props himself on his elbows. He stares at me, his eyes bugging so far out of their sockets they scare me, and his face as red as a turkey's waddle. Seems his nose, that spills over and onto his veiny cheeks, has grown even larger since the last time I laid eyes on him.

I step back, not daring to let go of my box.

"No one let me in, sir," I say. "I come all by myself."

My voice is quivering so I clear my throat, stand up as straight as a stick, and nod, like I'm as sure of myself as I can be.

"Hey, I know you," he says, wagging his finger toward my face. "You're that . . . that kid . . . that Hill kid, aren't you?"

I nod, my hands sweating so I nearly drop my metal box. I let go my hands one at a time and swipe my palms across my dress.

"Your daddy's trial hasn't come up. It's still going to be a couple of weeks yet."

"Yes, sir," I say. "I understand." I swallow hard, wishing he could somehow push his bulging eyes back in his head.

"Well then, why are you here? Can't you see I'm a busy man? Get on out of here now." He flips his hand at me, like he's flicking a fly in midair.

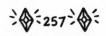

"Elsie! Elsie!" He stretches his neck to see into the front office. "Why does she always seem to run off when I need her? Elsie!"

He rubs his head with his hands.

"She gone. No one's out there," I say, glancing back over my shoulder. "But it don't matter because it's not them I need, and I'm not leaving until I talk to you."

"Now listen, kid, I told you, I don't have time. I'm a busy man. The last thing I need is—"

I sling my metal box up onto his desk, and I don't plop it down quiet either. Mama says the best way to let someone know you mean business is to make a lot of noise at it. And since I'm the one got us in this mess I'm the only one can get us out.

"Mister Sheriff Nix, sir," I say, not quite knowing what's proper to call the high sheriff, "I got something to tell you and it's important."

He grimaces, leans around me, and yells, "Elsie! Elsie!"

"Please don't call for that lady no more, sir. I saw her go down the hall with a stack of papers two months long. I'll be finished what I got to say long before she gets back if you'll just listen."

He slumps back in his chair and lets out a long, slow breath.

I walk around to the side of his desk so's I'm sure he can see me when I talk. My knees are knocking like the cut wheel of our wagon smacking the ground, and I'm feared they will give way at any second. I take a deep breath.

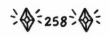

"I'm not quite sure how to say this so I'm just gonna spit it out, just like Daddy says I should."

"Go ahead, if you must. I'm listening," he says, leaning back and crossing one leg on top of the other.

"My daddy didn't steal nothing. He's innocent, just like he claims."

"Now listen, I've already told you—"

I interrupt, "But, I know who did steal that money."

He sits straight as a tree, his chair making a popping sound.

"Who did it? Was it the Negro? I knew it! I knew it was him!" He snaps his fingers like he's come up with the best idea since the Model T.

"No," I say. "It wasn't Mister Abraham, and I wish you wouldn't think of him like that. He's a good man that's been nothing but kind to us. Matter of fact he saved our lives once in a twister, but, please, sir, let me finish while I still got the nerve."

I let out a long breath and study the sheriff's face. He looks like he's ready to pounce, or jump to his feet, or maybe even go to shooting.

I swallow hard. "It was me," I blurt out. "I done it. I'm the one you want."

"Now listen here, kid—"

I prop my hand on my hip and shove the other one up in his face. "I'm not finished, sir." I'm aiming for him to hear every word I got to say and I'm standing in front of him so he can't get up and run 'til I'm done with what I got to say. "I stole that money."

He shakes his head and rubs his cheek with his hand. "You honestly expect me to believe you stole that money, and not your daddy or that Negro?"

"Yes, sir," I say, sounding just as sure and positive as I know how.

He shakes his head. "Why should I believe you? Why should I not think you're just telling me this so I'll let your daddy out of jail?" He leans so close it scares me.

Sunlight streaming in the windows on the side of his office catches the star on his shirt and flashes in my eyes, causing me to squint.

"'Cause I'm the one with the proof. It's right in there," I say, pointing to my metal box that I already plopped down on his desk.

His eyebrows raise, and he glares down at me with them buggy praying mantis eyes of his. There's a long, skinny string of spittle oozing from one corner of his mouth, and I wish to goodness he'd blow that booger from his nose.

But no way I'm going to tell him.

He pulls the box close and raises the lid right slow, like he's feared something's going to jump out and bite him. I wouldn't have thought it possible, but his eyes pop out even farther when he opens my box and lays eyes to that money. He looks at me and squints, his eyes disappearing into slits, but it's not long before he opens them up again.

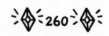

He slumps back into his chair and lets out a long breath, the kind you give when you're not sure what you're going to do next. I reckon he got himself together right fast though because he sprung forward, put his hands on his knees, and stared me right in the eyes. After that, they wasn't but one thing left to do.

38

On Account of a Ticket

"I told you I done it," I blurt out.

He slumps back in his chair again, crosses his hands in his lap, and glares at me. His face is gruff and scary, with a scowl that would scare a mountain lion from its den, and I don't mind admitting I'm fierce afraid of what's coming next.

"All the money's there," I say. "You can count it if you want. I didn't keep none. I want to give it back to the store."

Still, he just stares, looking me up and down and back again. It seems like hours he just sits, and gapes, and breathes. And the longer he sits, and gapes, and breathes, the stronger I'm feeling.

"I know I'm going to be arrested and I know I've got to go to jail. I'm ready," I say, not hesitating one iota with my words. "What I done was wrong and I know it, but I want to pay my debt to society and serve my time behind bars." I hold my arms straight out so he won't have trouble slapping on them handcuffs.

For the first time since I come, I see just the hint of a smile on his face. But, as quick as it come it's gone, and then he's gruff and mean all over again.

"So, tell me, Miss Hill. Why?"

"Sir?"

Now, I'm not dumb. I know what he's asking, and I know why I done it, but I'm just not rightly sure—yet—if I'm ready to tell him.

"Why did you do it? I mean, what was it you needed bad enough to steal for? A doll? A new book? A candy bar?"

I hang my head and swallow hard. No one in their right mind would risk being locked up in a jail for a doll or a candy bar, but there's no way I can tell him that I wanted the money to buy a train ticket to get back to my mama. Then on second thought, I reckon there's no way I can't tell him.

Whatever happens though, I'm tired of lying.

Lying's not done anything but get me in more and more trouble. Them lies got bigger and bigger with each one I told. They got me in so much trouble in fact, that after the lying come stealing, and it's the stealing that's going to send me to jail for the rest of my days.

Reckon there's nothing I can do now but blurt it out.

"It was all on account of a ticket," I say, hoping he won't ask for more.

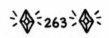

"A ticket? What kind of ticket? Were you running away from your daddy?" He leans forward, and this time he gets so close I have to take a step back. His breath smells like rotten cigars, old coffee, and garlic. I swallow hard, trying not to breathe. "Did he do something bad to you? Did he beat you or—"

"Naw, naw. Daddy's never done nothing . . ."

I stop in the middle of my sentence and listen to my voice, surprised at the words that are fixing to pop out, words about my daddy only doing good by us. Matter of fact, it's almost as if someone else is saying it besides me. For the first time I'm admitting what Abraham's being trying to tell me since he come. Daddy does take care of us. He sees to it we got clothes on our back and shoes on our feet, even if they do come from the church's ragbags.

He does his best to see to it that we eat. Oh it may not be all we want to eat, or what we want, but we do eat, and he makes sure we always stick together. Humph. Abraham's right. My daddy is a good man. Reckon I've just been too stubborn to see it all along.

"Go ahead, kid." The sheriff's words shake me from my thinking. "You can tell me the truth. Did your daddy do something to you that made you want to leave him?"

"No, sir. You're not listening to what I'm trying to say. What I want to say is, I was missing my mama—something fierce—and all I wanted was to get back to her. See, Daddy took us away from her—"

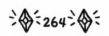

"Oh, so your daddy's a kidnapper? He stole you away from your mother?"

There's nothing I can say to that, because I reckon it's true. Daddy did kidnap us away from our mama.

The sheriff rakes his hands through his hair. From the looks of what little there is still left on his head, I reckon they's been a whole heap of young'uns in his office confessing to crimes they committed that their parents done got blamed for. He shakes his head real fast, like he's shaking ice cold creek water out of his ears.

"Listen, just tell about the part where you claim you stole the money, all right? Your mama will be here this afternoon. We'll sort out the business of the kidnapping after she gets here."

"Yes, sir. Well, I wanted to get back to Mama, to put our family back together again so's we could live all together, and be happy the way we was when Daddy was working the coal mines. We went into town back in Beaumont to buy supplies. Daddy and Abraham—"

"Abraham. That's the Negro that works for your daddy, right?"

"Yes, sir. I mean, no, sir. Abraham don't work *for* Daddy. I mean, he's no hired hand or nothing. He's really more of a friend. He works *with* all of us, singing and playing the banjo while the triplets sing and entertain the crowds. Anyway, Daddy and Abraham was in back of the store and the triplets was running around, scaring the life out of me because I was feared they would break something we didn't have money to pay for. That's when it happened."

"What happened?"

"I told you. I stole it. That's when I stole the money. I saw the money drawer open with all them bills hanging out and flapping in the breeze. I looked around the store. They wasn't nobody looking so I reached up, and snatched the money. I shoved it in my pocket and then ran all the way back to the wagon. I pulled out my metal box from under my cot and stuffed the money in it. I was going to use the money to buy a train ticket to get back to Mama, but, well, things just got all messed up. The flyers I drawed and nailed up in all the towns to show Mama where we'd be if she come looking led the lawmen right to our wagon. And folks blamed Daddy for something I done and now I'm here. And, reckon I'm ready now."

"Ready? Ready for what? You mean there's more?"

I hang my head and stare at the hole in the top of my shoe. "I'm ready to go to jail and serve my time," I say. All of a sudden I think back to Hazel's question about Daddy, and it 'bout scares the life plumb out of me.

I take a deep breath. "You're not going to hang me, are you?" I whisper.

The sheriff cackles. He laughs. I mean, he don't just snicker, he laughs a belly-jiggling, head-thrown-back, mouth-open-wide laugh.

And me? I just stand here.

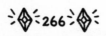

Watching.

And waiting, for what I'm feared will come next. But, I must admit, I do feel like there's a weight the size of a sack of coal that's just been lifted from my shoulders.

"Young lady, that's the most wonderful story I've ever heard in my life, and believe me I've heard quite a few." He wipes tears from his face with the handkerchief he's pulled from his back pocket.

I can't for the life of me understand why he thinks my confession to thieving is a wonderful story. Here I am, barely twelve years old, facing the rest of my life in a jail cell. Or worse, hanging, and he's cackling like a laying hen.

"Miss Hill, I know this is Texas, and in Texas, it's true, we're tough on criminals. But even Texans don't hang children— even ones that steal." He clears his throat and straightens up tall in his chair. And I realize the laughing he's done is over.

"Now. Are you declaring to me that you stole this money from the general store in Beaumont, Texas, and that you are not only confessing to the crime, but you're willing to return the money to its rightful owner?"

I think a bit on his words, wanting to be sure to what I'm agreeing. "Yes, sir," I say. "That's what I'm saying, just like you said it." I nod.

"Elsie!"

I turn, and there's Elsie, standing square in the doorway of the sheriff's office. She's much taller with no desk in front of her.

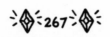

"Yes, sheriff?" she says.

He points to me. "This young lady has just confessed to a crime. Seems we have the wrong person in custody. Would you please take her to see Paul?"

"Yes, sheriff."

"Miss Hill, you've done a brave thing today. No, you've done more than that. What you've done by confessing is give your daddy back his life. If it wasn't for you he'd have spent a mighty long time behind bars. Now, I believe when the store owner hears your story and gets his money back, he just might consider dropping the charges. But while all that's fine and good, it don't satisfy me completely. After all, I've got the law to uphold, and one thing I can't abide in is children who steal."

He looks down at the gun laying across his desk, then he turns back to me with a look that says "You're gonna pay."

"If you was my young'un I'd see to it that you never thought about stealing—ever again. Matter of fact, around these parts we punish our children if they even look like they're *thinking* about stealing." He picks a pencil from a tin cup and beats out an unsteady rhythm on his desk. "Why, did you know there are places in this world that if they catch you stealing they whack off your hand up to your wrist?"

I gasp and swallow hard.

"Now, while I don't abide in whacking off body parts, I do have to see to it that the law is carried out and them that break the law pay."

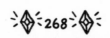

"Yes, sir. So I reckon you're going to lock me up in jail?" I ask, my voice quivering and shaking.

He drops his pencil and stares at me for the longest time without saying a word, and his look's not kind either. Matter of fact if looks was enough to whack off a body part, I'd be missing an entire arm.

"No. I'm not going to lock you behind bars, but when your mama gets here we're going to come up with a suitable punishment." He rubs his forehead with his hand like he's trying to rub my memory from his mind. "And we haven't even started to discuss the bit about the kidnapping. That's a whole other mess to get into."

He sighs and shakes his head as he looks me up and down like he just don't quite know what to do.

"You mean I won't have to go to jail?" I ask timidly, feeling a little smile come across my face.

"That's what I mean," he says. "I can't promise, but I don't see any reason the store owner would want to press charges. All he really wants is his money back."

I let out a long breath. I can't remember feeling this light-weight in all my born days. Matter of fact, if I was a bird I'd be soaring above the clouds right about now. The way I see it, there's not but one question still left unanswered, so I reckon it's my duty to ask it.

"Um . . . sir . . . does my daddy have to stay in jail?"

The sheriff smiles.

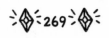

He stands and plants both of his big, wide hands on my shoulders. "Slow down, Miss Hill. Your daddy does not have to stay in jail, but he's not exactly free to go, just yet. We still need to talk to your mama about that. Now, it may take just a bit, but you go with Elsie and she'll do what needs to be done to clear this whole stealing mess up."

I look Elsie in the eyes and for the first time since I've come, she smiles. And I'm more than happy to smile back at her. Draping her arm across my shoulder, she leads me out of the sheriff's office.

"Oh, and just one more thing, Miss Hill," the sheriff says as we're walking out. "If I ever hear tell of you doing any more stealing, from anyone, anywhere, at any time, I'll personally see to it that you spend more time than you desire behind bars. Do you understand?"

"Yes, sir."

As Elsie's walking me from the sheriff's office, Anita Silverstone walks out.

"Chestnut," she says, "I wondered where you'd gotten to. There's someone in my office to see you."

I look her in the eyes and she's smiling from ear to ear. It seems even her eyes are dancing a dance of excitement. She nods.

"Why don't you go on in."

And I do. I run fast as I can to the office I saw Anita Silverstone come out of, and sitting there in a chair as big as the sheriff's is . . .

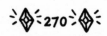

39

Finally!

M ama! Oh, Mama! I knew you'd come! I just knew it!"

I run like a rabbit and fall into her open arms, and it's just as I dreamed for two long years it would be. I close my eyes and lay against her pillows, trying my best to soak in the love I've missed all that time.

"I've missed you so much, Mama!"

I breathe in her scent and it's just as I remembered: perfume, talcum powder, and fresh-washed clothes, fluffed outside by the summer breezes, and all of it rolled up in such a pretty package as my mama.

She pushes me back, still gripping to my arms. "Let me look at you," she says. And you can believe I look at her too.

She's as pretty as I remember with laughing eyes the color of turtle shells and hair as dark and shiny as the crows that perch the clothesline in winter. Her skin is as fair and pale as

Hazel's baby doll, and her lips are painted the deepest shade of pomegranate red I ever did see.

"My, my, how you've grown!" she says. "Why, if I'd seen you out on the street, I wouldn't have known it was you. You're the prettiest thing I've laid eyes on in quite some time." She smoothes my hair with her hand.

Anita Silverstone strolls back into the office with a grin on her face wide enough to choke a baby crocodile. "Chestnut, do you know this lady?"

"Oh, yes, ma'am," I say. "This here's my mama. My sweet, loving, long-lost mama and I'm not aiming to ever let loose of her again." My smile is so wide it pains the muscles in my face. I grip Mama's hand with the both of mine, swing it back and forth, and kiss it over and over again.

"Mama, where have you been?" I stare up into her eyes. "Have you been searching for us? Did you miss me as much as I missed you? Oh, just wait 'til you see the triplets! They're not babies any more, why they're plumb—"

"All right now, Chestnut," Mama whispers, patting my hand nervously. "Calm down. Let's not get too excited. There'll be plenty of time for questions and answers, later."

Her face flushes red as a poppy flower and I notice right off she's not looking into my eyes. She's looking to Anita Silverstone the whole entire time that she's talking.

Strange.

Reckon she's just as feared of folks in the lawman business as I am.

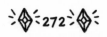

"Oh, Mama, I've got so much to tell you," I say, "and wait 'til you see our wagon!"

Mama rolls her eyes to Anita Silverstone. Humph. If I didn't know better I'd say Mama's embarrassed of me. But that can't be. I reckon she's just tired from her travels.

"How was your trip down?" Anita Silverstone asks.

Mama dabs at her forehead with her handkerchief. "The train ride? Dreadful! Simply dreadful. All of the stops we made in those tiny little one-horse towns full of insignificant little people going about their silly little lives. I've never been so cramped for so long a time in all my life. Folks say the train is the way to travel but I don't agree. There are just too many people crammed into one place to ever call that comfort!"

Mama's changed.

I ain't sure how exactly, but she's changed. I listen patiently as she spends more time complaining to Anita Silverstone about everything from the train ride to the shoes she's wearing that are causing corns and bunions where there used to be tiny little toes.

After a while of Mama's complaining I suppose Anita Silverstone must have gotten a-fierce tired. "Chestnut," she says, "would you like to take your mama outside under the oak trees and wait for your daddy to be released?"

"Yes, ma'am," I say. "Oh, Mama! Daddy's going to be so happy to see you."

Mama shoots me a look as she snatches up her purse and plops it over her arm like a wet towel to a clothesline. Been

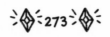

so long since I been with a lady carrying a purse I 'bout forgot what it looked like. Then again, Mama always did say a lady never goes into public without her purse—even if there's nothing in it of substance.

Walking the halls from the sheriff's office, my face is aching from the grinning. I stare up at Mama and think again just how pretty a lady she is. But, I can't help but think again how Mama's changed. She's smiling and nodding and speaking to every lawman in sight. Now it almost seems like she's one of them, with her shoulders pulled back and her nose sort of high up in the air.

We stroll, arm in arm, to a small grove of oak trees just outside of the building. The sunlight is shining down around Mama like a light's been turned on from Heaven. She's dressed in the prettiest blue suit I ever did see. Reminds me of the robin's eggs in the nests up and under the eaves of our barn. With her purse hung over her arm and carrying her white gloves in her hands, Mama looks right citified, just like the ladies in the fancy shops in Louisiana.

"Oh, Mama," I say. "I forgot something inside. I'll be right back. You wait on me now, you hear?"

Mama smiles and nods but I'm not quite sure if she's nodding and smiling at me or that lawman just passed.

Anyway, I left my metal box back in Sheriff Nix's office and I'm not aiming to leave it behind. That box cost me a cut on the finger when I dug it out of the ground with a rock back at the coal mine.

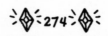

I run lickety-split back into the building thinking all the time I'd better hurry or Mama will think I'm not coming back. Elsie's there, behind the desk, same as always, but this time she smiles when she lays eyes on me.

"Miss Elsie," I say, "I forgot my box." I spit the words out fast because I don't want to miss a minute with Mama. The whole time I'm standing before Miss Elsie I'm stretching my neck, weaving and bobbing, trying to see outside, to make sure Mama don't leave.

"Your box? Where did you leave it, do you remember?"

"Yes'm. I left it in Sheriff Nix's office, on his desk."

"Oh, all right. I'll get it for you," Elsie says. She plops a book down on top of her papers and turns back toward the sheriff's office.

"It's metal. And black," I holler, as she walks away. No way I want her to bring me back the wrong box.

There's more folks coming and going in this office today than the last time I was here. Way I got it figured it must be a right busy day for crooks.

It's not too long before Miss Elsie returns, carrying my box in her hand.

"Thank you, ma'am," I say. "I appreciate it. Oh, and don't take me wrong, ma'am, but I sure do hope it'll be a cold day in May before I ever lay eyes to this place again."

Elsie's eyes disappear into slits, and she chuckles.

I quickly lift the lid on my metal box to make sure it's empty, tuck it up under my arm, and take off running down

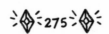

the hallway to the door. I'm dodging lawmen and criminals, men and a few women, to get back to my mama fast as I can.

Closer I get to the doorway though, the louder the sounds are from the outside. Sounds like someone yelling. Sounds like a woman's voice. Matter of fact, it sounds like my mama.

40

More Than Money

When I get to the door there's a crowd gathered just beyond the steps.

I see right away who's doing the hollering.

Mama.

She's standing face to face with my daddy and she's giving him a what-for-whipping. The words coming from her mouth aren't nice either. They're loud, and curt, and hateful and I can't believe what I hear her saying.

"You're a no-account man, Slim Hill! Never have been, and you never will be."

My first thought is to go and get in the middle of them.

But I don't. I can't. Seems when there's trouble the last thing that wants to move on a body is their feet.

Reckon she has a right to be angry, him stealing us away and all. Still, this is not going a thing in the world like I had it planned, and I don't rightly know what I can do to change it all.

"You're a lousy, good-for-nothing dirtbag!" Mama yells. "How could you do this to me? I'm a lady of importance in my community. I don't have time to be running halfway across the country to tend to you and your *problems*." She's wagging her finger in Daddy's face so close that Daddy's having to squint and duck to keep from getting hit.

I'm surprised at Mama's anger, but I guess I shouldn't be. It was just as I'd thought all along. Daddy stole her babies away from her. Of course she's angry.

"How in the world did you get yourself into trouble like this anyway?"

Daddy, staring at the ground, shrugs. Then he lets out a deep breath, then cocks his head to look at Mama.

"No, sir, don't you go looking at me like this whole thing is my fault. You're the one who made it impossible for me to stay by refusing me the finer things of life that I deserve."

Mama takes a breath, looks around at the folks that's gathered, and rolls her eyes. But it don't take her gathering more than that one tiny breath before she sets in to letting Daddy have it again.

"You only have yourself to blame for this, Slim. I wouldn't have come in the first place but the sheriff made it seem like I had no say in the matter."

Daddy's gripping his hat so tight his knuckles are white. His shoulders are slumped and round and the more I watch what's happening between the two of them, the more I realize he's not saying anything back to Mama. Not a word. Matter of fact, he don't even look at her. He just stares down at the ground hanging on tight to his hat.

The crowd is growing and folks are scratching their heads, and I know they're wondering what in the world is happening. Daddy's as pale as a water lily in the noonday sun, and Mama's face is as red as a rhubarb stalk, but Daddy don't say a word. Not one little uttering sound does he make. Daddy always says a real man will treat a lady with respect no matter what the circumstances. He's as respectful of Mama now as I've ever seen him be even though she's giving him more than the dickens, and I realize standing there in that mob of nosy busybodies that's gathered that my daddy's more of a man than I'd ever come to recognize.

Mama leans in toward Daddy, pointing her finger up next to his nose and waving it around in his face.

"And another thing," she says. "I have a new life now. I'm a woman of high society. What do I want with a bunch of babies running around, worrying the life out of me, tugging at my dress-tail? I'll not have it. I'm going back to the city where I have a real life, with a man who's sophisticated, with a place in the upper class. I told you the day you left that I wanted a very different life than the one you were offering me. How much plainer can I be? I don't want those children. Not then, not now, not ever."

All of a sudden, my legs are so weak they won't hold me up and I drop right straight down to my knees, like I was fixing

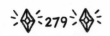

to do some praying right there in front of the sheriff's office. I gasp for air, feeling like I just been slapped in the chest. Hard.

"The day I left you was the best day of my life, and I've no desire to go back to that life. You just take your little nut farm, Slim Hill, and leave me alone, you hear?"

She turns from Daddy and walks away, but before she gets too far she hollers back, "Leave me alone."

Mama walks down the street, toward the heart of town and I watch 'til she's clean out of sight.

I don't know whether to cry or throw up, but before I do either I look over at my daddy. For what I reckon is the first time in my entire twelve years of living, my heart's breaking into tiny slivers for him.

He lifts his hat to his head and pulls it down low over his eyes. His head's hung plumb down to his chest and his shoulders are stooped and bent. He buries his head in his hands.

Folks standing around are whispering, punching each other with their elbows, and pointing. Some of them are snickering, like they think maybe my daddy got just what he deserved, but I know better. Daddy don't deserve the way Mama done him. Nobody deserves that.

I stand and pull my metal box close, square my shoulders back, and stiffen my upper lip so's I don't dare let Daddy see I'm choking back tears for him.

I move close beside him but I ain't sure what I can say that will make it better. I reckon sometimes the best thing a person can say is nothing at all, so I just slip my hand in his

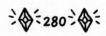

and grip it as tight as I possibly can. For the longest, we just stand under the grove of oak trees without talking at all, my daddy's head hung way low.

After a while I take in a deep breath and muster the courage to look up into his eyes. They're wet, and dripping a steady stream, like the water pump behind the house back in Kentucky. Daddy's face is the color of wood ash from the morning-after bonfire and his hair is mussed and unkempt.

"Daddy," I say, quiet as I possibly can, just like him when he's fierce mad and upset. "I'm sorry Mama done what she done."

A tear falls from Daddy's cheek and drops right down into the hole on top of my shoe. I don't say a word, but I look up at Daddy, to see if he saw it too. He looks at me and all of a sudden, there's a smile runs across his face and mixes in with the tears. His Adam's apple bobs up and down and I know he's swallowing back a cry.

"Daddy, there's something else," I say, still holding to his hand and rubbing on his arm. "I'm sorry I done what I done. I know stealing is wrong and I should have told the truth about it from the beginning. It was all my fault that you was thrown in jail."

Still, Daddy don't say a word. Tears roll from his cheeks even faster now, like river water off mountain rocks, and he's trembling and shaking from the crying. But still, I just stand there, holding his hand real tight.

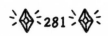

After a while he lets loose my hand and lays his hat on the ground. He pulls a wrinkled handkerchief from his back pocket and wipes his eyes. He blows his nose too, real loud, and looks around to see if folks are still standing and gaping. Some are, but most of them are gone by now, thank goodness.

"Say, Daddy," I say grabbing hold to his hand again, "there's something else I want to tell you, I mean, while I'm talking, that is. These last two years I didn't believe you about Mama's leaving. I mean, I always thought you stole us away. Now I know better. I been wrong all this time about Mama. I had no idea about her, Daddy, and I just want to say—"

"Stop," he says, through the tears and just as quiet as a church mouse at a funeral. He lets loose my hand, turns to face me, and gently sets one finger to my lips. "Just stop. I'm sorry you heard the things you heard. You didn't deserve it. You're a beautiful young lady and a fine, fine daughter. No man could ask for better than you are. I'm so very proud of you." He squats in front of me, then leans in and kisses me gently on the forehead.

"But one thing I won't have you do, Chestnut, is disrespect your mama. The two of us might not see eye to eye, but she gave you life and don't you never forget it. And the triplets don't need to know their mama didn't love them enough to stay with them, so what say we just keep all this between the two of us, all right?"

"All right, Daddy."

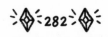

"And there's something else—while we're getting stuff out on the table," he says. Daddy wipes his face with his handkerchief. He takes a deep breath and then lets it out again, like the worries he's been keeping bottled up inside are beginning to disappear.

"I realized when I was locked up in there that I'd been expecting a lot out of you—too much, really—and I want you to know I'm sorry," he says. "You're a young lady, sure, but you're still a little girl too. You deserve to make your own friends, have some fun, and do some more growing. I'm sorry that I've kept you from that by dragging you across the country chasing my foolish dreams."

Daddy smiles and I stand there in front of him realizing what a mighty big man he really is. And I understand too, how wrong I've been about him. But there's one thing I've not been wrong about and I reckon now's as good a time as any to set the record straight.

"Daddy," I say, my shoulders squared and a deep swallow in my throat. I look him right in the eyes so's he knows I mean what I'm fixing to tell him. "I don't want to lie no more."

Daddy nods.

"I mean it. I don't want to lie about the elixir, or about having a sick grandmaw, or none of that. I don't want to cheat honest, God-fearing folks out of their money, and I want to tell the truth from now on, even if we don't do so good with the elixir."

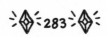

Daddy hangs his head and stares at the ground for the longest time. Any other time I'd have the fear in me too, afraid of the tongue-lashing he's ready to cut loose on me, but not now.

Not anymore.

Leastwise, not about this.

"Lying's wrong, Chestnut," Daddy says, looking me in the eyes and smiling sadly. "And I should never have asked you to lie, no matter if it's just stretching the truth, or a little white lie, or a big old red-hot one, it makes no difference. Lying is lying and it's wrong. Always. No matter the reason. I was wrong to ask you—to teach you—that it was all right. I'm sorry." He stops and watches me. "Will you forgive me?"

I nod.

"Tell you what," Daddy says, standing, "like I said before, I did some thinking of my own while I was locked behind those bars. What would you say if I told you I think you and the triplets and Abraham and me should stop selling the elixir altogether?"

"You mean it? But how will we get by? I mean, how will we make a living?"

"Well, I don't think Abraham would mind going back to New Orleans," Daddy said. "He's bound to still have lots of contacts there." Daddy raises his eyebrows and a big old smile come across his face. He wipes his eyes with his handkerchief, then tucks it into his back pocket. He put his hands on my shoulders again.

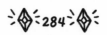

"I was thinking maybe we could buy us a little house, one that sits right out next to the ocean, where a young girl can stick her toes in the sand, feel the waves slap against her legs, and sketch and paint just as long as she sees fit."

I gasp. I can't believe what I'm hearing. I thought he didn't know nothing about my dreams. It's almost as if Daddy's been reading my mind all along, and that's worth way more than money.

"I could get a job, and the triplets could sing with Abraham on the weekends, when school's out. What would you think about that?"

Right then and there, in front of the sheriff's office and county jail in Dallas, Texas, I realize the truth. What I've wanted all along is a loving family. Oh, it don't matter if it's not a mama and a daddy, but a real family, where a girl can dream—daydreams and night dreams—all she wants, and a home where she knows she's important and loved.

And it seems to me, that's exactly what I've got.

Matter of fact, reckon it's been here all along. I was just too stubborn to see it.

"Say, Chestnut," Daddy says, smiling down at me with the warmest, kindest, biggest chocolate-colored eyes I ever did see. "What say we go get the triplets and Abraham and Old Stump and have ourselves an elixir busting party?"

And I say, "You know what, Daddy? I reckon you know best."

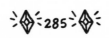

Acknowledgments

This author wishes to thank:

My agent, Sally Apokedak, for believing and encouraging from the beginning, and for the hours invested teaching such a "greenhorn."

My editor, Adrienne Szpyrka, for loving Chestnut and the gang as much as this writer.

My writing buddy, Kirsten McDonald, who tirelessly reads, rereads, and then rereads again. Thank you for not killing off any of these characters.

And finally, my critique group, The Story Weavers of Asheville, for comments and suggestions that helped improve this story.

About the Author

A lover of mountain cultures and lingo, Lisa Fowler has lived her entire life in the shadow of the Great Smoky Mountains in the quirky, sometimes downright peculiar city of Asheville, North Carolina. And life with three wacky dogs and one exceptionally talented and beautiful daughter is a constant reminder that things are not always as they seem.